HARDISTY'S TOWN

It was a devilish two-pronged plan which succeeded. But a man was killed in Commoddee, a once lawless town that had been tamed by the notorious killer-marshal Max Hardisty. Ruthless and determined, Hardisty was soon on the owlhoot trail once more. The hunt was on for a bunch of rustlers and a pair of killers. Action exploded in the canyons and badlands, but Hardisty never faltered. The name of the game was vengeance — and murder.

Books by Vic J. Hanson
in the Linford Western Library:

KILLER ALONE
SILVO
KILLERS' HARVEST

VIC J. HANSON

HARDISTY'S TOWN

Complete and Unabridged

LINFORD
Leicester

First published in Great Britain in 1996 by
Robert Hale Limited
London

First Linford Edition
published 1998
by arrangement with
Robert Hale Limited
London

The right of Vic J. Hanson to be identified as
the author of this work has been asserted by
him in accordance with the
Copyright, Designs and Patents Act, 1988

British Library CIP Data

Hanson, Vic J.
    Hardisty's town.—Large print ed.—
Linford western library
    1. Western stories
    2. Large type books
    I. Title
823.9'14 [F]

ISBN 0-7089-5276-3

Published by
F. A. Thorpe (Publishing) Ltd.
Anstey, Leicestershire

Set by Words & Graphics Ltd.
Anstey, Leicestershire
Printed and bound in Great Britain by
T. J. International Ltd., Padstow, Cornwall

This book is printed on acid-free paper

For Frances — with love

1

THE massed herd was like a rippling sea of brown, hides gleaming in the hot sun. A sparkle from long horns going slowly up and down as the cattle grazed and rested. It had been a long drive. It had been the biggest herd that Bill Dakell had ever driven and he was mighty proud of it. But he had to leave it for a while. Now was payment-time.

As he mounted his horse, his foreman Tod Millen came to him on foot. Dakell bent from the saddle.

"I'll be in the hotel," he said. "Room Four. You be there at one o'clock, y'understand?"

"Surely, Mr Dakell. I'll be there on the dot."

"I'l be on my way then."

Dakell nudged his horse who started obediently forward. His rider set him at a steady trot and the ranked buildings of the town called Commoddee began to appear out of the heat-haze.

Dakell hadn't been there in a long time and the place looked to him to be bigger. But he would have expected that. There was good land around here and a creek a little way back where the cattle had already watered. Commoddee had once been kind of wild, but it had better law now and, as Dakell had heard, a fine community spirit.

Pretty soon he was leaving the horse at the livery stables and walking along the boardwalk at the edge of the bright, dusty Main Street to the hotel, easily seen, its sign swinging in a small breeze.

Superbe it was called. Kind of a grandiose moniker. But the place wasn't half-bad at that. Clean and spacious lobby bright in the sun's rays. And Dakell was lucky, for the proprietress was behind the desk and the rancher had known her from way back in

2

different circumstances. He called her 'Miss Nita'.

"Hallo, Mr Dakell," she said and held out her hand, which he took.

Her grip was strong and firm. She had red hair and a pretty face from which brown eyes twinkled. He didn't think she'd changed much, whereas he had, his thinning hair shot with grey, his gunbelt too tight across his belly.

"Everything's fixed," she said. "I'll take you up to your room."

She came from behind the desk, moving like a young girl and, as if on cue, an oldster came from behind there, nodded, took her place.

She let Dakell go first up the stairs and he was a little peeved about that: she was beginning to look better to him all the time.

The room was at the back and out of the glare of the sun. It was clean, cool, inviting.

"I'll wash up first, Miss Nita," he said. "I've got somebody calling at

3

one o'clock and want to see 'em up here . . . "

"As you wish, suh."

"So I'll stay here till then an' rest."

"Prime," she said. "Bathroom right next door."

"Thank you."

"You're purely welcome, suh."

She left the room. God, the way that woman moved! Polite as all hell also. Like the town, she had changed. But he'd heard things . . .

He shrugged his bulky shoulders and made his short way to the bathroom.

He was lying on his back on the bed, still fully clothed but a whole lot fresher, when the door was rapped. His gunbelt with the well-worn but finely kept Remington pistol in its long holster, was draped over the back of an elegantly shaped mahogany chair at his side. He got off the bed and stood upright and then he was even nearer to the gun. He called, "Come in."

A florid-featured man of about his own age but with a greying

4

handlebar moustache came in, asked, "Mr Dakell?"

"That's me."

"I'm Smithon."

"I figured . . . " But if that was the beginning of a sentence, Dakell didn't finish it, for there was another man suddenly appearing behind the first one.

"My foreman, Jed Spokes," Smithon said hastily.

Well, that figured as well of course, didn't it? "Welcome gentlemen," Dakell said and the two visitors came further into the room, the second one, Spokes, dangling a small burlap sack in his right hand.

The door was rapped again and there was another entrant as Dakell gave the word. And then he added, "My foreman, Tod Millen, gentlemen."

"Howdy, folks," said Millen.

He had a pair of saddle-bags over his shoulder. He took them down and slung them carelessly on the bottom of the bed. They were obviously empty.

"Cattle's ready," Millen said.

"We spotted 'em," said the other foreman, Spokes, and he tossed his sack on the bed beside the saddle-bags.

Dakell bent and undid the drawstrings on the sack, opened the top, glanced inside.

"Count it," said Smithon.

"Did you count the cattle?"

"Hell, no. Ain't been all that near."

"Transfer it, Tod," said Dakell and, moving to his side, the young man took bills and coins in handfuls from the sack and spread them into the two saddle-bags, weighing them in his hand before he slung them over his shoulder again.

Dakell handed Smithon a paper. "Bill of sale."

"Thank you, suh. We'll collect the beef right on."

"My boys will help if you need 'em."

"Thank you, suh."

Polite as all hell!

★ ★ ★

The drive had been a good one with no great mishaps. Drovers and cattle were tired, resting while the boss and the foreman had gone into town. When they returned there would be a pay-out and the boys could hit the town but had been told most strictly that they mustn't overdo things, particularly the regular hands, if they wanted to keep their jobs that is.

Waddies who had been taken on just for the drive would probably want to go their own way as soon as they'd collected their pay, so then Bill Dakell would have no control over them. They'd been well picked, though. Besides, the marshal of Commoddee was one Max Hardisty, a man who'd turned a wild town into a blustering but eminently peaceable and *wider*, more prosperous one. Bill Dakell had known Hardisty briefly in the old days and had learned since that the renowned town-tamer hadn't changed much, had only gotten older and more astute than ever, and that was something all right!

While Dakell and his foreman Tod Millen were in Commoddee the boss-man in camp was Dakell's old friend and sometime partner, veteran Texas Joe Elliwell, a cantankerous old cuss who stood no sass from anybody. Even so, most of the boys who'd worked with him for a considerable time revered the old son-of-a-gun, but took great pains not to show it.

Money on the hoof, and the chuck-wagon and other rolling stock; and the horses in the remuda watched over by a yellow-haired boy called Snowbird; and a campfire and the smell of coffee and cigarette smoke wafting in a soft breeze under the broiling sun. Peace withal. And who could have imagined that at this time anything could happen to spoil things now?

If drifters or wandering tame Injuns picked at the edges of a herd they did this stealthily and by night . . .

Young Snowbird was the first to see

the bunch of riders and they seemed to be coming away from town, if sort of obliquely. The yellow-haired wrangler didn't really pay them much attention. He thought that out of the corner of his eye he saw one of them wave and he tipped back his wide-brimmed hat, but all he got was the sun in his eyes. He couldn't watch them as they got to the edge of the herd which was furthest away from the camp.

Their plan had been a daring one. A ploy of utter surprise. They started by shooting their guns in the air. They were good herdsmen. They worked the beef. The stupid longhorns allowed themselves to be roughly manipulated by the horsemen on their tractable steeds, intimidated and terrorized by the sudden noise of the guns exploding on the still air.

Some of them went off at a tangent. The riders evaded these for, despite their expertise and that of their cayuses, theirs was a perilous undertaking and could lead to a bloody mess.

But it didn't . . . The leading steers were wheeled, their horns tossing, glinting in the sun. Their eyes rolled, their mouths slavered. They were suddenly as one. More than they'd ever been before they were creatures of stampede.

The rustlers fired guns again and screamed and some of them took off their hats and waved them, and those flickering things, appearing to the cattle like darting birds, sent them into frenzies of retreat. Nothing could stop them now. And some of the rustlers began to fire their guns back in the direction of the camp where men had risen, started forward. They'd been taken completely by surprise and many of them didn't have weapons handy, scrabbled for them now.

It was a shambles. Nobody was hit on either side and the stampeding herd and its new keepers were going like the wind as, now, the ranchmen, toting rifles and handguns, ran for their horses. Young Snowbird was overwhelmed, wrestled

10

with tie-ropes, yanked at tough rawhide and swore.

"Stay here, kid," said Texas Joe Elliwell as he mounted his own rawboned grey mare.

"All right," said the kid, nodding dumbly.

He was still nodding, almost in bewilderment, as the riders with old Joe at their head streamed away from him. But now he began to shake his nervous cranium, lank yellow locks flopping over his boyish brow. Those goddam cow-thieves and the herd they'd rustled had a hell of a start, they surely had!

2

BUYER SMITHON and his foreman Jed Spokes had gone and, watched sardonically by his boss, Tod Millen had unbuckled his saddle-bags and was counting the money.

He'd finished, and said, "It's all right," when the door was rapped.

Bill Dakell had his hand on his gun-butt when he called, "Come in." And at the same time Millen had refastened the bags and dropped them at the foot of the bed behind him.

Proprietress Nita's head was popped around the edge of the door as it was opened and she said, "The dining-room's still open if you gents want some chow."

"We'll be down directly, Nita," said Dakell.

"All right." She withdrew.

"That's some kinda woman," said Millen.

"She'd eat you alive," said Dakell. "Besides, last I heard she was Marshal Max Hardisty's woman. And Max's the sort who looks after his own — an' then some."

The door wasn't knocked again but they both saw the knob turned, heard the pad of feet. They weren't perturbed, both figuring that it would be Nita again, who'd forgotten something, maybe wanted to tell them just what was on offer downstairs in the dining-room.

The door swung open wide this time, though. Then the two new male visitors were able to march in almost abreast, both with levelled guns in their hands.

"Easy, my friends," said the first one, who was just a tiny bit ahead of his companion. "One abrupt movement an' we start blasting. Just raise your hands slowly over your heads an' come forward just a mite."

Neither Dakell or Millen had suicidal

tendencies. They did as they were told. And the second man skirted them carefully, came in behind them and collected their hardware.

The second man hadn't said a word. His partner spoke up again. "Spread out," he said. They spread out. "You," he pointed with his free hand at the younger cowman. "Kick them saddle-bags over towards me. Easy now. *Ee-eeasy.*"

Millen, though his handsome face was dark with rage, didn't put a foot wrong. These two hold-up characters were obviously professionals who knew exactly what they were doing. The young foreman kicked the saddle-bags forward as if he was kicking eggs and, with his free hand, the talky outlaw picked them up and looped them expertly over his shoulder.

His partner, though he hadn't taken the two ranchmen's gunbelts, had managed to tuck their guns into various parts of his own belt. He pointed his own gun at the two fuming victims and he grinned at them, still wordless but with an almost affability. He was towheaded and not much older than foreman Tod Millen.

The other man, older, hatchet-faced and swarthy, spoke up again. "Turn round, both o' yuh."

"Can we put our hands down?" Dakell asked.

"You can put 'em on the top o' your heads . . . Now get down on your knees."

"Goddam it, why . . . ?"

"Do as you're told or, begod, you can have worse than that."

They got down on their knees and, when they were told to do so, flopped from there on to their bellies. Millen hit his head on the foot of the bed and swore obscenely.

"Stay just like that," said the tormentor. "We're goin' now, but if we hear any sounds from here we'll blast through the door.

The footsteps retreated. The key was obviously taken from the inside of the door and transferred to the other side, turned. By this time Tod Millen was moving. "Hold it," said his boss but the young foreman took no notice.

His long length was eel-like. He raised it. He moved for the door. The door was locked on the outside — he must have known that. But his almost mindless fury carried him swiftly and, he must have thought, noiselessly.

There was a sound like cannons going off in the hallway, a hideous, echoing cacophony in that enclosed space. The slugs tore through the panels of the door, spraying wood chips.

Millen caught two slugs directly in the chest and was knocked backwards by their power. Dakell was rolling; and Millen hit his boss's legs with his own tottering feet and was thrown over on to the bed. He rolled over on his back, his hands clawing at air, then his legs jerked out to their full length and he became still, his dead eyes staring glassily into nothingness.

Outside, footsteps padded in quick

motion down the stairs and then the sound died and there was a great silence only broken by the creaking of boards as Bill Dakell hauled himself to his feet. It was those creaking boards that had given Tod away. Dakell gave a little sob as he bent over the boy who'd been like a son to him. There was nothing he could do for Tod any more.

He moved over to the door. He heard footsteps approaching; there was a sound of a key being turned in the lock. Then the door was opened.

It was the oldster who had helped Nita with the desk in the lobby. He said, "I saw two men run down the stairs an' out. One of 'em nearly knocked me over at the bottom o' the stairs. They were strangers. I found the key on the stairs . . . "

He paused. He was looking past Dakell and at the bed.

"Oh, sweet sufferin' Jesus," he said.

★ ★ ★

There was the sound of more footsteps in the passage. A tall man appeared in the open doorway with a gun in his hand. Nita was just behind him.

The tall man seemed to take in everything with a sweeping glance as he halted.

"Marshal," said the old desk-clerk. "I saw 'em. Two of 'em. Nobody I know."

"All right, Gabe. I saw two riders going away as I came to the hotel — after I heard shots. I didn't have my horse, didn't know what was going on. Go downstairs, will you, an' stop anybody else from coming up?"

"Right." The old man scuttled away.

The marshal turned to Nita who stood with one hand up to her mouth. "Anybody else on this floor?"

"Jack, the hostler. But he's at his job now o' course."

The tall man looked at Bill Dakell and spoke his name.

"Hello, Max," said the rancher. He half-turned. "This is my foreman Tod

Millen." There was pain in his voice. But he went on, "That pair stuck us up for the cattle money. I hadn't seen them before."

"I didn't see them," said Nita. "I was over by the window when they went out. I was in the back o' the house when I heard shots. I wasn't sure of the direction. I didn't see the two men come down the stairs but I heard the horses. They must've gone the opposite way to where I was lookin'."

"Go get the undertaker, Nita."

"I will." The girl left.

"I'll cover Tod." Dakell yanked the sheet from beneath the body then made of it a shroud, a complete cover.

There were more footsteps on the passage. It was old Gabe again, but there were two other men right behind him: rancher Smithon and his foreman. "I tried to stop 'em. But they . . . "

"All right, Gabe. Don't let anybody else up. Use a shot-gun. You've got one, ain't you?"

"Yeh."

"Anybody would be intimidated by a shot-gun. Go!"

"All right, Marshal." The oldster scuttled away again.

Smithon said, "We stopped at the hostler's." He jerked a thumb in the direction of his foreman, Jed Spokes. "His hoss had a stone in his shoe. We were in the stable when Jed said he thought he heard shots . . . "

"I did!"

"I didn't. But I'm kinda deaf in one ear. And old Jack didn't hear anything . . . But almost right after Jed had spoken two horsemen rode by goin' fast. We didn't get a look at 'em, though. Then when we came out we saw folks gathering at the hotel and we came back." Smithon lost words, pointed dumbly at the shrouded form on the bed.

"They killed Tod," said Dakell. "And they took the cash we had from you. They must've got information."

"Where would they have got information?"

"I don't know."

"I'll get a posse together," said Marshal Max Hardisty.

"Yes," said Dakell vehemently.

"We'll come," said Smithon.

"Me too," said Nita.

"You'll stop here, my lady," said Hardisty.

"I can shoot as good as any of yuh. Better maybe."

"I know. But it's best if you stay here. Bear with me."

The undertaker arrived, a gent taller than the marshal — with a wall eye. He said he'd look after Tod. The rest trooped downstairs. Old Gabe wanted to join them. He already had his trusty shot-gun and folks in the lobby were arguing with him. Hardisty told Gabe to stay where he was at, look after Miss Nita. He picked men who volunteered.

Seven horsemen — with the leader, Hardisty, making eight — left Commoddee under the red of the sun. At least they knew which way those two killers and robbers had taken.

3

THEY could vaguely hear the sound of the stampeding cattle, like the rumble of a distant summer storm. But they couldn't even see the tail-ends of the beasts, or see their dust, or smell it.

The chuck-wagon cook was half-Indian and a good tracker. The leader, Texas Joe Elliwell halted the boys and the cook, who was called Moosehead, got down on his knee and pressed his ear to the ground. He was a man of few words, didn't use any now, rising, giving them their direction with a sweep of his arm like a general urging his troops onwards.

"They've got a hell of a start," said Texas Joe. Seemed like he'd used those words before. Moosehead nodded his cranium under its battered felt hat with an eagle's feather in the side.

22

There was a low range of hills ahead. Texas Joe said he thought maybe badlands ran behind them, and Moosehead agreed with him, said the signs were there. The sun was going down and the light wasn't as good as it had been. Moosehead got down to cut sign again. But then he said, "They'd have to go through them hills, unless they've veered off, and that don't look likely."

"Yeh," said Texas Joe. "As I remember there's quite a wide pass through them hills. They'd have to channel the beef through that."

Moosehead had just used more words than was his custom. He now reassumed the guise of a drug-store Indian and rode sedately on. And the hills were nearer, clearer.

The sudden crackle of rifle-fire sounded like a barrage as the echoes caught it, carried it grotesquely. It was just two shots fired simultaneously

Yes, the cattle would be going like the wind, the rustlers having to strive, men and horses, to keep up with the snorting longhorns till they spent themselves out. The men would have to keep them together as best they could which wouldn't be hard until they began to slow down, drift. But by then some of them would want to rest and the leaders would have to be forced on, with the hope that the others would follow docilely.

Oh, those cow-thieves would lose a few all right! But, even so, the rest would be a prime herd, and still a big one.

They had been fast, that bunch — and they'd been clever. No attack. Nobody hurt. A daring ploy; a calculated stampede. A big risk, but one that seemed to have paid off so far.

They were in New Mexico. At the rate they were going and if they kept in the same direction that Moosehead had indicated they would soon be in the wide plains of Texas, and Texans just purely loved cattle; and some of 'em weren't too particular how they got it either.

Although the drovers — either regular hands or waddies taken on for the big drive — didn't know this of course, there had been murder and robbery in the town called Commoddee, one of their friends, a colleague, a fine ramrod, was dead, and their boss was on a vengeance trail. They didn't know that the once-notorious killer called Max Hardisty, now marshal of Commoddee, was the leader of the posse and riding side by side with boss Bill Dakell. They were tracking too, of course, just as the cowboys were, only the posse had a tougher job, had nothing to go on at all.

Only one thing seemed pretty certain, was peculiar to both pursuits unless one or the other, or both, was suddenly changed by the pursued — the trail was leading towards wild Texas territory.

Then again, there was one thing that the posse knew that the drovers maybe didn't: before getting to the Texas border they had to cross a stretch of badlands, a bare, rocky terrain with wide acres of sand and then rock and then sand again and, in all of it, very little vegetation.

The cattle wouldn't like the look of these lands which, could be said, were of little use at all to man or beast, except for a few snakes and lizards. There wouldn't even be hawks and vultures in the flat skies, for prey, either alive or dead, was hard to come by.

The cattle would have to be kept running or they would falter and some of them would die in those unwelcoming and evil lands. They would have to be terrorized to keep them running to the other side where they could smell water and grass.

But two killers on two fleet horses and provisions and the incentive of the rich haul on their saddles would be able to get across that great expanse and leave less sign than cattle would — maybe no sign at all.

though, from sharpshooters spread apart. And one of them was pretty good.

Moosehead went '*Ug*' and fell from his saddle, rolled.

"Spread out," yelled Texas Joe.

The boys reacted, scattered, Moosehead's horse among them. Texas Joe came from his saddle, got down on one knee beside the half-Indian cook who said, "They got me in the leg."

Blood was already coming through one leg of his pants and staining the sparse grass as the man struggled to rise.

"Stay down," said Texas. He turned to a rider near, whose horse had been startled by the shots and was acting up.

"Help me," the older man said and the feller got down, whipping his bandanna from around his neck. Between them they fixed Moosehead up as best they could.

The two sharpshooters had opened up again. But now the rest of the ranch crew had dismounted and sought

27

what sparse cover there was: humps in the ground, a rock here and there, a lone cottonwood behind which a single hand had managed to hide himself, the muzzle of his rifle poking out.

Fire was being exchanged. Didn't look like anybody else had been hit.

"Take Moosehead back to town," Texas said to his young helper whose horse had settled now, shooting or no shooting, and was watching the two helpers and the man on the ground curiously.

"Take him to the doc," Texas went on. "Find Mr Dakell as well an' tell him what's happened. I should've done that right away I guess — but there didn't seem to be time. Snowbird an' that other feller will be lookin' after the camp." The 'other feller' was a young waddy who'd been taken on for the drive, who'd pitched from his horse and busted his ankle, had only been able to sort of hobble around since, doing odd chores, had attached himself to the yellow-haired wrangler who was even younger than he was.

With help, Moosehead was struggling to his feet. "My horse," he said.

"We'll get him for you," Texas said. "You go with Aldo now."

"Yeh, you get in my saddle front o' me," said the young ranny. "I'll raise one stirrup an' you can rest your laig in that."

The young man's horse seemed to be taking his part now as, between them, Texas Joe and Aldo made Moosehead as comfortable as possible.

Texas raised himself higher to watch them go and dropped again as a slug almost took his hat off. He was further away from the hills than the rest of the boys, but he certainly wasn't out of range of the snipers in the rocks up there.

They'd obviously been left behind to harass the pursuers, and they were doing just that.

They seemed to be roughly one on each side of the beginning of the pass leading through the hills. There were plenty of rocks piled there and they could make a quick getaway. They could probably get way out without being seen, after dramatically slowing down the ranch posse that was tailing them and their pards and the stolen herd.

Texas Joe spotted a small outcrop of rocks ahead of him and scuttled crablike forward. Nobody took a shot at him this time. He crouched down and surveyed the terrain.

All the boys — including himself now — seemed to have found some kind of cover. He saw their movements, one by one. None of them were worryingly still, so if there had been hits, Texas had to assume that they were minor ones.

The milling horses had no cover, though — and that fact was brought home to the watching man now as the riflemen in the hills opened up again and one of the ranch beasts squealed in agony and went down, kicking, then becoming still.

Texas Joe came to his feet — half-crouching, weaving, his pistol held in front of him.

Some of the other boys spotted his movements and began to make some of their own, crouching, weaving, sending blistering fire up at the hills, the rifleman behind his tree covering them, and a good shot he was too, even if he couldn't see anything to shoot at.

But the two marksmen in the hills had found their cleverest ploy now, were probably a mite peeved that they hadn't thought of it before. They sent more shots at the horses, not actually hitting another one — the beasts had shied away from the corpse of their late companion — but scattering them. Two of them broke away and high-tailed back in the direction of the distant camp where there was no beef now, and only two horses there belonging to wrangler Snowbird, and the young waddy with the busted ankle.

Men ran to try and retrieve the

fugitives and one was caught, held. But the other went like the wind — and rifle-bullets spat around beasts and men. Then the firing died as men sought cover again.

There was comparative quiet. Then a drover who was crouching down nearer the hills than anybody else, shouted, "They're moving, I heard 'em."

Men and horses regrouped. The runaway steed was let to go now: there wasn't time to try and catch him. His rider had Moosehead's mount to take his place — and the boys pushed on, warily at first but then with more haste as they hit the mouth of the pass, the sound of their movements echoing around them. There was no sun and these were the places of shadows.

They had left a dead horse behind and a runaway who would doubtless find his way back to town or to camp. Other mishaps were but minor. One flesh wound in a man's left arm; a gash in another man's forehead where a sliver of rock had caught him. The rifleman from behind the tree had a newly pockmarked face from fragments of bark that had been thrown into it, a near-miss by the opposing sharpshooters. Another feller had a bruised knee but he'd gotten this from falling clumsily when he scuttled for cover.

Yeh, the boys were pretty good really . . .

4

IT was almost dark when the young cowhand called Aldo and his wounded companion, Moosehead — two men on one horse — hit Main Street of the town called Commoddee.

By this time Moosehead was making heavy weather, alternately passing out, then coming partially aware and mumbling to himself in a mixture of English and a dialect that Aldo couldn't understand, had never heard from the leathery-featured chuck-wagon hand and tracker before.

Moosehead's pants leg was sodden with blood which had seeped from the broken wound as the jolting pace of the overloaded horse shook coverings free. Aldo knew that the wounded man had lost too much precious life's blood. He made for the doc's place right off, although he sensed from things around him, bustle, questioning shouts, that something bad could have happened in town lately, he couldn't figure what.

The doc, a Civil War veteran who'd seen all kinds of wounds, quickly took Moosehead in hand. "I think he'll be all right, son. He's as tough as an old bull buffalo."

"All right, Doc. But — but has something been happening in town?"

The doc told Aldo what had been happening. When Aldo heard what had befallen foreman Tod Millen, his eyes saddened and he uttered a soft curse. Though not much older than Aldo himself, Tod had been the ramrod, and a stern one at times. But the young ranny had liked and admired the man. To be killed so suddenly, so uselessly: it didn't bear thinking about!

Aldo left the medical office. At first he thought of going to the undertaker's to pay his last respects to his friend Tod Millen. Then he decided that there would be no use in that: looking into a dead face that would be nothing like the usually cheerful face he had known, speaking words that couldn't be heard, would have very little meaning.

Better to try and avenge Tod's death — hell, the money didn't matter, and not even the stolen herd now as far as Aldo was concerned. And he figured he had to go out after the posse. And, besides, boss Bill Dakell was with the posse, and old Texas Joe had told Aldo he had to find the boss and tell him of the thing that had happened; *that other thing*.

Like the old doc had said, bad things seldom came singly and if there was a second, maybe there'd even be a third. The ol' doc certainly had a kind of lugubrious sense of humour.

Aldo left his own horse resting up and feeding with Jack, the old hostler who ran the stables in Main Street. He told Jack he wanted a fast horse, and why he wanted a fast horse. The wizened oldster chose for him a lean paint with a wicked eye.

"Fastest cayuse I've had for ages,

son. But don't turn your back on him or he'll bite your ass off. Just make him know who's boss that's all."

"Yeh, he's gonna take me where I want to go or I'll beat his ears back," said Aldo. Even if you had a lump in your throat you had to cover it with a corny joke.

"Wisht I was goin' with you, son," said old Jack wistfully.

He watched the boy go on the paint who seemed to be behaving himself right well so far. The boy's got sand, the old man thought. Maybe that awkward cayuse's instincts had told him that. And he liked trouble too . . .

★ ★ ★

It started like a rumble of distant thunder. But there was no lightning; no sheet lightning even. And in the bottom of the pass now there was darkness and the men had to guide their horses carefully.

Shale began to patter and the horses

became restless. These small signs were the first intimation of what was going to happen. And then the sound from above them became a cacophonous roar.

"Forward," screamed Texas Joe. "Move . . . Gallop!"

But the terrorized horses were already in flight over the uneven ground, the men holding themselves desperately in their saddles. And the beginning of the deluge started to hit them. The stones and rocks, the small boulders like missiles thrown by a giant hand. The horses seemed to be ploughing through snow. But the shale and debris was more hurtful and frightening than snow.

The pass had narrowed at this point but it had been wide enough to let the cattle through. And they would have been through by daylight, their pace slowed. They would be free now, none of their members left behind, no sign of their passage.

Now the darkness was absolute. If

a man looked upwards to the top of the chasm he had been able to see the stars past the pinnacles as pinpricks of light high in the sky. But now there was nothing and riders hunched in their saddles with their heads down and their bandannas pulled over their mouths as if in a dust storm. But this was worse than a dust storm.

It was no natural mishap either: that was evident. The rustlers had had a plan all along and this was the horrendous culmination of that.

The marksmen. The chase. The narrow part of the pass. And even the darkness had been on their side.

Men at the top, hidden, out of harm's way themselves: men to start this avalanche.

A man, hit in the head by a rock, pitched from the saddle. His screaming horse was thrown on top of him. They had been driving forward to try and beat the fall: that had been Texas Joe's ploy. But it hadn't been quick enough. It didn't work. No man knew what was happening to the rider who had been knee to knee with him, and now the horses were wild, suffering things.

The fall stopped more suddenly than it had begun and there was a pall of silence only broken by the pattering of dust.

The pass was blocked. Horses and men began to back out, some of the men on foot, some of the horses riderless, the horses snorting, the men coughing with streaming eyes as the dust still swirled around them in the blackness. They couldn't see the dust, but it was like a pall. They couldn't see much at all.

A man grabbed a horse's reins and, for his pains, was kicked in the knee and collapsed, groaning. He had fallen at the feet of one of his comrades who reached down, helped him to drag himself backwards out of harm's way. But they, bruised and shaken though they both had been, were two of the lucky ones.

A man was calling weakly for

help. Another one was making strange gasping noises. But these died to a pitiful rattle and then he was silent.

The dust began to waft away and men peered into the darkness, straining their eyes. They began to feel about them and their whispered cries were like prayers.

Texas Joe Elliwell clambered to his feet, his head swimming. He raised a shaking hand to his brow and felt the sticky blood from a very nasty gash he had sustained. A snorting horse was near him. He didn't know whether it was his own horse or not. Probably not. A coughing fit seized him, passed. He pulled his bandanna up over his mouth where it had been before.

The horse had shied away from him, but he found it again, gentled it with his hands and with the soothing tones of his voice while his head thudded as if Indian drums were beating in his brain.

He heard the sounds that pierced his heart. He began to try and look around him.

5

THE job had gone like a heavy, high-priced hunter on a golden chain. A chain that led to riches, for neither of them had ever owned a golden hunter, or any other timepiece of any great note. Off and on, they hadn't done too badly and sometimes they had lived for a while pretty high on the hoof. But they'd never been actually rich — not until now.

There had been no mishaps — except somebody who'd been told to keep still had been heard to move prematurely and shots had had to be flung through a door. They didn't know whether they'd hit anything or not, and they didn't care.

The younger, tow-headed one was called Rip, had been 'Rip' ever since he was a wild orphan sprig. His partner, and his senior by about six years, was swarthy and hatchet-faced and was called Black, just 'Black'. Neither of them answered to anything fancier.

They had run with a gang for a while until after an abortive bank raid when the rest were killed or captured — the latter, a pair of partners, being subsequently hanged. Rip and Black were partners, too, by then and they were the only ones who escaped a vengeful posse. They'd had no share of any loot and had hardly a bean between them.

Now they had more beans than they'd ever seen before and were riding fast and good, not to say high, wide an' handsome. By dark they decided to rest their horses awhile. They hadn't seen or heard any signs of pursuit. They had a long ride still ahead of them and were willing to take a chance, have a break, some eats, some cold coffee that they had in their canteens, some sustenance and a blow for the horses. They would pick up further mounts later but had seen no sign of being able to do this yet.

The luck had been with them lately all right. They'd gotten information and they'd worked on it fast. And the whole caper had paid off right handsomely.

Neither of them had a timepiece. But they figured that they'd taken about fifteen minutes break and both they and the horses were raring to go when they came out of the outcrop of misshapen rocks that had sheltered them. It was a dark night and that was all to the good.

The stars were high in the sky but there was no moon and Black said it was likely there'd be rain before the morning came. But they'd expect to be in the dry by then. The night was warm but there was a cooling breeze and they'd be able to gallop the horses again.

If you hit a lucky streak you have to go with it: any gambler will tell you that.

But you have to guard against getting

too cock-a-hoop, getting sloppy or careless or both, getting arrogant, thinking that this wasn't a lucky streak after all but a product of your own brilliant planning. If you got too cock-a-hoop, yessir, that's when Lady Luck is likely to turn around on you and spit right in your face.

When the rattlesnake had heard the vibrations in the ground he had been dozing in smooth sand half-hidden by a boulder that was warm to his hide.

Humans! And those four-footed monsters they bestrode!

Probably they'd go right by.

But they didn't.

They stopped. They skittered about as if they had been bitten by something. They should be so lucky! They finally kind of settled down. But one of the men almost sat on the rattlesnake, used his rock as a leaning place. Even then the snake didn't react as he might have done. He was an old snake and kind of tired. He heard the voices and they were quite soothing and he smelled the smoke and the food and that wasn't unpleasant. He must've dozed again.

When the interlopers started to move, that was when he became irritated. The man who had blanketed him in his small sandy bivouac rose very suddenly as if he had a journey to make. He kicked sand with his heels and he almost kicked the snake.

The rattler — the sidewinder — well, he reared up then. He reared back. And then he struck with all his force, burying his fangs in the flesh of the calf of the now-standing man, burying the fangs deep just above the rim of the riding boot, wickedly, drawing them out then slithering away, out of the sand, out of the rocks, moving off, side and swing, *side and swing* into the night.

Black — for it was he — gave a hiss of pain and clutched at his calf, almost pulling himself over in the process.

"Christ," he said. "I've been bit."

"God," said Rip. "I thought I heard a sort of rattle."

He had risen more smoothly than his partner, and more silently, and was now standing upright.

"I didn't hear anything," said Black. But maybe he'd been making too much noise.

His leg gave way under him suddenly and he sat down.

"It was just above my boot," he panted. "The pain's shootin' upwards."

"Get the boot off," said Rip, and he got down on one knee before his partner while the two horses looked on curiously.

Black's panting got louder and he was little help as Rip yanked at the boot which finally came off, precipitating the young man backwards and momentarily startling the horses. But they came forward again. This was something new. And what strange sounds that man was making now!

The sounds abruptly stopped. Black

fell back, head thudding dully against a rock.

Rip looked at his partner's face in the pale starlight to which his eyes had become accustomed as the two men rested. Black stared up at him balefully with shining eyes, but eyes that had no life in them at all. Black's mouth was open in a rictus of agony and white foam ran from one corner and down under his chin.

"A rattler," said Rip softly to himself. "Had to be."

Nothing moved around him. Even the horses seemed to be still. Rip peered. Must've been under the big rock there, under the sand where there was a depression. But nothing lay there now, nothing moved.

Rip reached down and closed the lids on Black's dead eyes.

It was while he was still bending that he heard soft thudding from the earth. Horses approaching in the distance. Had to be! He'd thought that Black and he had stayed here a mite too long. But he'd gone along with the older man as he usually did.

He worked fast. He stripped Black of all his accoutrements.

The saddle-bags with the money were on Rip's saddle — Black had gone along with that — so their transference wasn't necessary. Rip lifted Black's body on to the back of the man's horse and the beast snorted, jittered a bit. Maybe he could already smell death.

"Keep still, you jackass," Rip told him but said it in a soft, gentle tone of voice, and it worked.

He was able to tie the corpse on the saddle with Black's own *riata* of long, tough rawhide. He used the end of the rope and lashed Black's hands round the horse's neck and, after using his knife, with another piece of rawhide tied his legs under the horse's belly.

"You're ready for Christmas now, ol' pardner," he said as he turned the horse in the direction he desired and gave him a sharp slap on the flank, then bending and picking up stones, residue from the rock outcrop.

He threw hard, pelted the horse's flank, sending him like the wind into the night, not back, not forward, sort of semi-crosswise. He couldn't explain it to himself in his mind but he figured he knew what he was doing and was doing it right.

"Keep on goin' like you're goin', hoss," he said.

He made sure he had all Black's gear on his own horse which he forked, and rode fast in the direction Black and he had been taking.

The posse — if that was what it was — would be nearer to him now he thought. He could only hope that maybe they wouldn't hear his mount's hoofbeats which cloaked anything they might make now; hell, he didn't have any time for listening himself an' that was a fact.

He veered off at a tangent. Keep 'em guessing, he thought.

Maybe the posse would go the way

he wanted 'em to go. Maybe it wasn't a posse after all. The thought amused him and he chuckled to himself . . . The luck hadn't stayed with Black, but maybe it would go along with little ol' Rip from now on.

6

THE pass was blocked. A man and a horse lay buried under the rocks and couldn't be reached. Another man was dead. They would be able to carry him home. His horse had to be shot, was left where he had fallen. Another man was pulled from under a horse as the beast struggled to his feet. Maybe he'd been stunned, but he seemed all right now. His rider certainly had been stunned, came round cursing and spluttering.

There were casualties all around and some of them would have to be seen to as soon as possible.

"We'll have to get out of here," Texas Joe said. "We have to take stock." A master of understatement was phlegmatic Joe.

"We'll have to go back," said another man.

But then Joe led the way back from the drifting dust and the carnage. The sound of the horses' hooves and the chink of bridles and spurs was the only sound then; and a mocking echo as if whispering voices were jeering at the sorry cortège.

★ ★ ★

Despite the ropes that held it, the body had slumped sideways in the saddle and looked like nothing more than a badly filled sack of oatmeal. The horse wasn't running any more but standing trembling, looking back over his shoulder and surveying the bunch of riders and cayuses with eyes that rolled in the night. But he didn't balk when the Smithon foreman, Jed Spokes, dismounted and approached him, even seemed to welcome the man, nuzzled him as Spokes stroked his flank and muttered soothing words.

Only a cursory look was needed at the horse's burden. "He's dead all right," Spokes pronounced.

Marshal Max Hardisty let out a string of mainly obscene pronouncements of his own then added, "We've been tricked . . . Cut 'im down."

Spokes took out his jack-knife and did some slashing and stepped back and let the body fall. He was joined then by his boss, Smithon, and by Hardisty and Bill Dakell, the man who'd collected a big slice of money from the other rancher in exchange for a prime herd.

The money had been stolen and Bill Dakell's own foreman, Tod Millen had been murdered. In all probability the dead man on the ground had been one of that pair of robbers and killers. It would have been a damn' miracle had he had the money with him. In fact, he had obviously been denuded of everything of value except his horse and saddle, and they'd been left for a cunning purpose.

Hardisty got down on one knee before the corpse and said, "He don't look pretty. I reckon a rattler got 'im, can you believe that? I guess it happened at that outcrop of rock where they seemed to have bivouacked. There are two vaguish trails from there, higgledy-piggledy. We took the wrong one. We follered the wrong horse."

The tall man rose and looked about him. He pointed. "There's a clump o' rocks over there. Stick him under 'em."

The job was soon done. Then the bunch turned about.

Suddenly their leader held up a hand, halting. They all clustered behind him, heard the hoofbeats.

"One rider I guess," said Hardisty.

They waited, all with their fists on the butts of their hand-guns.

The rider appeared out of the night under the pale starlight, saw them, reined in with a skidding of hooves on the soft grass.

"It's Aldo Boner," said rancher Bill Dakell. "How, what . . . ?"

The young ranny's words came in

a gabble. "The cattle's been run off, boss. In plain daylight. There was shootin' later an' ol' Moosehead got hit. I had to take him back to the doc's in Commoddee. Texas Joe told me to tell you — I had to find you . . . "

"The others . . . ?"

"As far's I know they still on the trail o' the rustlers."

"This territory's gone mad all of a sudden," said Dakell dully.

"Join us, Aldo," said Hardisty.

"Yes, Marshall." Aldo became part of the posse.

They talked among themselves as they rode at a steady pace. Only their leader was silent, his tall frame erect in the saddle. He was an action man and could be completely ruthless. But he was a thinking man also: they all knew that.

It was clear that Rancher Smithon wanted to get back to see what had happened to the herd he'd bought. And Rancher Dakell wanted the money that had been stolen from him, wanted revenge on whoever had killed his young friend Tod. One miscreant was finished, buried under rocks in a shallow grave. But the other one was still on the loose, and he had the money, there was little doubt of that. And he could be to hell and gone by now or in a nest which he figured he might feather at his leisure, and he had the *dinero* to do it with all right now.

Hardisty spoke up at last. He sounded kind of sour but his words were plain. "I guess we better go back to Commoddee."

There were no arguments, not even from Smithon or Dakell, no matter what either of them might be feeling — and maybe the former had the best of it. He would at least be able to find out whether his herd had gone the way of the money he'd paid for it, or not: there was a chance there maybe.

★ ★ ★

Texas Joe Elliwell and his bunch were back at the camp where the young wrangler Snowbird and two other hands had waited for them. The bruised, beaten and bedraggled manhunters had an horrendous tale to tell. There was one who would never talk again, would be buried and words said over him. There were others who were bad enough to be taken to see the doc in Commoddee, and this was the first thing to be laid on after there were things done to them in camp that would succour them temporarily.

"It's time Aldo Boner got back," said Texas Joe. "Hell, I thought he'd be here already. He only had to drop Moosehead off in town. I hope Moosehead's gonna be all right. Ain't Mr Smithon and his boys been here either?"

"No," said Snowbird.

"That's mighty strange. I expected the Smithon boys at least would've been here to collect the herd. And

58

that foreman maybe, feller called Spokes . . . "

"There's been nobody. And them boys you mentioned would've had a helluva surprise if they had turned up, wouldn't they?"

Another man chipped in on the young wrangler, voicing something that must have been on all their minds by now. "Mebbe somep'n happened in town."

Texas Joe said, "I'm going with the two boys who're takin' the hurt folk to Commoddee. Rest o' you boys stay here."

The small bunch set off. By the time they got to town everybody else seemed to be back and shock and speculation was rife.

★ ★ ★

Max Hardisty had a lot of questions to ask himself, had to try and give himself answers too, and that was the harder part.

He was the law here, and now things seemed to be coming at him from all sides. The territory that he'd tamed, had been proud of, had suddenly turned into a place of horror and mystery.

A robbery and killing. A rustlers' cattle stampede and its manufactured tragic aftermath.

Were these two things in some way connected or was it all a terrible coincidence? Whether or not, it seemed to Hardisty that in both cases the perpetrators of these crimes must have had prior knowledge, prior information even. And now he had to face the fact that the best place — and the most likely — they could have gotten information was right here in his town of Commoddee.

They had what might be called a council of war, and they all looked at the marshal. They held the council in the cleared-out dining-room of Miss Nita's Superbe Hotel and everybody notable was there.

Bill Dakell, who had lost his herd.

Rancher Smithon, who had bought it and lost it for, after money changed hands, the herd hadn't been Bill's any more. And now the money had gone also. Smithon's foreman Jed Spokes was there — and Dakell's elderly sidekick Texas Joe had turned up with a bandaged head, bringing more misery and mystery. Young Aldo Boner was there and other members of the posse, though some of those were still in bed.

Hardisty's friend, little, fat, astute Mayor Mobane was there. Leading citizen of Commoddee, he'd once been a drummer selling ladies' doo-dads — until he ran into Miss Nita and Hardisty and a mess of trouble. But that had been in the old days.[1]

The only individual missing was Hardisty's capable middle-aged deputy

---

[1] Hardisty, Nita and Mobane were introduced in *The Plains Rats*

Gil Tally who was up-country visiting a mighty sick relative. It had been all right for Gil to leave his post, and Hardisty hadn't even put somebody temporary in his place. The marshal hadn't dreamt that the whole territory was about to sort of blow up right under his chin. Gil wouldn't be back till Thursday at the earliest, so there were still days to go. Later than that if the relative, an uncle, handed in his pail.

Taking another posse out was a dim possibility, Hardisty figured. Could he get another all-fired keen posse together again and, if he did, where in hell would he take 'em?

Young Aldo Boner had volunteered. So had Jed Spokes, Rancher Smithon's foreman. Stolen cattle or not, Smithon still had a ranch to run, and his regular herd and crew. He said he'd spare Jed though, if the marshal wanted him.

Smithon figured he wouldn't see the stolen herd again. He was being all-fired philosophical about it, seemed like. Bill Dakell had said he'd reimburse his fellow rancher, the buyer, even give him the money back. They wrangled about this. Hardisty figured they'd work something out eventually that would suit them both, and he didn't worry his head about that right then.

He, too, was inclined to take the view that the herd was gone, would be sold, and then probably mingled with some Texas beef . . . But there might be a chance to get the rustlers. And the remaining killer with the money, whether part of the same set-up or not.

These were very tired men, some of them not nearly as young as they used to be. Hardisty made his plans, agreed to some things, vetoed others. Then, on his own, he ranged the town asking questions. But he got no answers of any great interest.

He went back to his apartment at the back of the jail and there, though he hadn't actually invited her this time, Nita joined him. Yeh, he was tired he said — but he had time for her. They made love, and then they slept. And when he awoke in the bright, early morning she had gone and somebody was knocking on his door.

Two people. Two tough young men raring to go, their horses waiting. Aldo Boner and Jed Spokes, his new deputies.

"I'll be right with you," said Hardisty.

It didn't take him long.

7

RIP had ridden hard and for a long time. It wasn't months, wasn't even weeks, but it seemed that way. He hadn't seen or heard any more signs of pursuit and he figured that both he and his mount needed a break.

He reckoned that the posse had taken the wrong trail, followed a dead man on a fast horse.

He paced his horse; over to the left of them there was a range of low but craggy hills. He knew a pass through there, a hell of a short cut. But he hadn't intended to take it. Over to the right of them, although he couldn't see it as it lay in a valley was a small settlement that he knew pretty well. It was away from the main trail and the pass and like a forgotten mudhole that the buffaloes had left. It was an outlaw roost.

Rip turned his horse slightly, a fine beast who reacted to his every touch or small spoken word. But a tired horse now.

They went a short way and then descended into the valley, seeing the clustered buildings of the settlement below them in the morning light. They hadn't bivouacked yet and it was more than time that they did: even the loaded saddle-bags, the riches, seemed to have become unnecessarily heavy across the saddle.

Annie will be there, Rip thought. He had lain low with Annie before. Her cabin, and the prime chickens she reared in the run, and the vegetable garden lay in a good spot at the side of the narrow tortuously winding creek. This was shallow and dried up in the summer so that water had to be found by digging in the earth. Right now it was narrow and very sluggish.

Annie's cabin was in a prime position for yet another reason. From three sides you could see the rim of the valley, though not the distant hills. But, if you kept a lookout, you could see anybody approaching, coming down the grassy slopes to the settlement. On the fourth side any visitor would have to come through the houses and unless a horse or a man were ghostly — or both of them were — you could hear them approaching. No grass in the so-called streets, just iron-hard, beaten earth.

Rip knew it was inevitable that he was being watched from some place as he guided his horse down the sometime slippery gradient. He crossed the narrow wash and his horse's hooves didn't sink very deep.

He hadn't crossed directly in front of Annie's cabin as that would have meant ploughing through her vegetable garden and coming too close to the wire-enclosed chicken run. The back of the cabin faced the stream. Rip went around and back aways and approached the front door which looked out onto what could be called, laughingly 'main street'.

He dismounted, left the tired horse with his reins dangling, and knocked at the stout door. There was no reply. The door was locked. Drifters were in and out of here all the time and it wasn't wise to trust anybody. Rip knew Annie had a cache but he didn't know where it was, in the cabin, or in the small outhouse; or even some secret place with the chickens or the vegetables.

The main window was closed tightly. Rip went round the side of the place and paused, looking back. There were folks moving about but nobody seemed to be taking any notice. And the narrow side window was slightly open.

Rip was not a big man. He was adept with his hands. He got the window further open and climbed through.

He was in the bedroom of the sprawling one-storey cabin.

Rip had been in places far more scummy than this one. One thing you had to say about, pretty, tough-as-boots Annie, she was neat.

Rip moved cautiously into the bigger, main room with the spacious kitchen running off it at the side and leading to the outhouse and from there to the privy. Annie's place was one of the few buildings that had a privy so close, most of them having to share outside structures that looked like upstanding coffins and creaked and squeaked protestingly when being used.

Suddenly Rip stopped dead in his investigating perambulations. He cursed loudly. He had left the saddle-bags with their rich contents outside on his horse.

Hells bells, he must be a damn sight more tired than he'd even thought he was.

He was galvanized into action again and now he moved a lot quicker. The front door! That was locked on the outside of course. He cursed loudly again, retraced his steps. The side door had a key on the inside which he turned after crossing the kitchen. Then there was the outside; then a sort of canopy of sagging timber overhead, and the privy. Then the horse, who was startled out of his doze as his owner descended suddenly upon him.

The man grabbed the bags. An old-timer was staring at him curiously from down the street. To hell with that mossyhorn! The man, toting his saddle-bags, went back into the house the way he'd come out.

Saddle-bags dangling in his hand Rip stood in the middle of the living room and stared owlishly about him.

He bent and put the bags under the deal table, then he went outside again, using the same route as before. When he returned he had his rifle. He had everything of value now.

Outside, the horse had looked as if he wanted to lie down and rest forever. In this land a horse was a valuable commodity too, worth its weight in any gold. He'd have to see to that horse, Rip reflected. But still he remained for a little while in the middle of the room as if he didn't quite know what to do with himself.

Black and he had had a rendezvous later. If the job had gone off properly that is.

The job had gone off properly all right. But there'd been a terrible sting in the tail, a sidewinder had seen to that — and Black was no more. Had the posse found him by now? If so, had they buried him, or had they left him for the creatures who loved dead human flesh?

Black had sort of led the way — but Black wasn't here to do that any more. Since Rip had worked his little scheme with Black's horse and Black's body, Rip had been going along on instinct. His ruse to throw off the posse had been a rare brainwave. And it looked as if it had worked.

Rip had never been a thinking man before, he'd always left that to others, to Black, for instance.

But now Rip had to think for himself. And, suddenly, to his own great amazement, he was beginning to do just that.

But, for the moment, he had to think of Annie too. Where the hell was Annie anyway?

He got the saddle-bags back from under the table and with them in one hand and rifle in the other he moved into the bedroom.

★ ★ ★

"So this is where Texas Joe an' the boys came to grief," said Hardisty.

"There's a dead man an' a dead horse under there," said Jed Spokes.

"Well, we can't do anything about that now."

"We can't get through either," said Aldo Boner. "We'd need a team of horses, rope an' tackle an' more men."

Nobody argued with this. And Hardisty said, "The trail led here. But which trail? We'll have to go round."

But, for the moment, all three of them seemed to be lost, staring at the carnage in front of them. This had once been a pass through the hills, this spot the narrowest and most awkward spot maybe, but now a nothing: what had been once a route to the Texas-New Mexico borderlands was now a tortuous rocky barrier, and would certainly have to be cleared as soon as possible.

"C'mon," said Hardisty brusquely and he turned his horse about, pushed it through the other two riders almost as if they weren't there, pushing them to the wall. The shale clattered. The dust drifted.

Here it was still dark and it was as if, suddenly, they wanted to get away from this accursed place. They pushed on with Hardisty in the lead and soon they were out in the pale morning sunshine.

They had come fast, but now was time for another pause and they were silent, somewhat despondent, as the leader, who knew this country pretty well, got his bearings.

8

RIP looked under the bed. The bare boards were clean. No dirt floor for Annie. No dust either. Elsewhere in the room, beside the bed and under the window and by the door, there were rush mats.

Rip got down on his belly and poked at the boards, even thumped them somewhat petulantly. There was no creaking, no particular hollowness in the sound. Rip straightened up again and looked around him, his rifle and the saddle-bags at his feet.

He crossed over to the window, bent, moved aside the mat. He stamped on the floor. Pretty firm. He got down on one knee and inspected the boards.

He reached to the long pocket in back of his belt and got out his jack-knife and opened it. He prised a couple of boards up at the base of the window

74

and next to the log wall. The boards were fairly short and his task wasn't too hard.

The soil was black and there was a smell of must. The nails were rusty but short, and there weren't too many of them. There was space, too, for the saddle-bags as he lay them out flat, neatly.

He put the boards back into place, knocked them down with the butt of his hand-gun. He decided that the floor then looked pretty much as it had before. He put the mat back in its place.

He looked around the room again somewhat bemusedly, hoping he'd done the right thing. That was a hell of a lot of boodle!

He heard the key turn in the door of the other room, the door open. He had pouched his hand-gun, but he kept his rifle tilted in his right hand as he crossed the bedroom, went through the door. Annie stood in the middle of the living-room and stared at him in astonishment. Then her expression cleared, became a welcoming one, and she exclaimed, "Rip!"

Then puzzlement set in. "How did you get in here?"

"Through the privy," said Rip, laconically. "How've you bin, honey?"

"All right. You?" Without waiting for his answer she moved towards him, at first tentatively, then in a rush, her dark hair flying around her pretty face. He caught her in his arms, his voice muffled as he said, "I've been all right too, I guess." Her mouth closed over his. But then they wasted no more time on preliminaries and he carried her into the bedroom.

The outer door was closed but it wasn't locked: more eager things were at hand: it had been a long time . . .

Rip had kicked the bedroom door to with his heel; before he took his boots off that is. So they both heard the bedroom door creak as it was opened. But they hadn't heard the man open the front door or any sound of him as he came swiftly across the floor. He had a gun in his hand. "My, my," he said.

"Lafe," cried Annic, for she saw him first.

Rip rolled quickly off her and almost landed on his ass on the mat. He reached for his gunbelt on the chair but then froze with his hand half-poised.

"Goddammit? Lafe. You scared the pants off me." He laughed thinly, nervously.

The other man, older, taller, thinner, with lank red hair and steel-rimmed spectacles laughed more immoderately, said, "So I see."

Rip was as naked as a newborn heifer. Annie had been the same but had now covered herself with the flimsy bedclothes. "Lafe," she said, "why in hell didn't you knock?"

The thin man didn't answer this question but asked one of his own. "Where's Black? I expected to find him here as well."

Rip sat on the edge of the bed with

unbuttoned shirt on and one leg in the air as he struggled to don his long johns. He remained in grotesque suspended animation as he queried stupidly, "Why would Black be here?"

"If Black's not here why would you be here then? You were together, weren't you?"

"Well, yeh . . . "

"What's goin' on?" demanded Lafe. He hadn't holstered his gun, and now he jerked it in his hand.

"Put that away," said Rip weakly. But Lafe didn't do this.

"Where's Black?"

Then Rip was thinking fast. His words came out in a spur-of-the-moment rush. "Black ain't here. He high-tailed. We got the loot but he double-crossed me. He double-crossed us all. I don't know where he is."

It was Lafe's turn to look stupid. But he didn't lower the gun. He wasn't that stupid. His eyes behind the spectacles were startled. But they were wary also.

"Come away from that bed an' that

gunbelt, Rip. Move."

"I ain't tidy yet. I . . . "

"Move I said." Lafe jerked the gun menacingly.

In his stockinged feet and with one leg of his pants half-down, Rip hopped away from the bed.

"You, Annie," said Lafe. "Get hold of that gear by the belt — do it very carefully — an' sling it along the floor to me."

"All right. I don't know what this is all about. I ain't seen Black myself in a coon's age — an' even Rip's been kinda neglecting me."

One of the girl's arms came out of the bed, and one sweet and globular breast, as she followed the thin man's instructions. Then Rip's armoury was at Lafe's feet and he kicked it behind him with his heel and through the bedroom door where, in his lecherous haste, Rip had left his rifle also.

Lafe was transformed now. When he first came in, levelled gun or not, he had looked not unlike some kind of professor in riding togs out for a pasear on a gentle steed. But now there was a sort of bottled tension about him and the eyes behind the spectacles had bright, cold light in them. Now Lafe looked like what both the other man and the girl knew him to be: a killer.

"Sit down on that chair at the side of Annie in the bed," he said, looking at Rip.

"All right, but . . . "

"Move!"

Rip shrugged, moved and, looking more presentable now, placed himself in the chair as ordered.

With his gun still levelled at the two people, Lafe leaned against the doorjamb. Annie sat up in the bed against her pillows but had covered her nakedness again. Her pretty, pugnacious face was now full of lively interest. "All right, Lafe," she said. "I'd like to know what this is all about."

"Black arranged to meet me here — and have Rip with him, of course."

"He didn't tell me that," burst out Rip.

"He didn't have to. He was in charge of the job. And, according to you, it went off all right, didn't it?"

"Yes."

Rip was cogitating again. Yes, Black had been the leader of the two of them anyway, and he'd always been a close-mouthed cuss.

Annie said, "I didn't know Black was supposed to come here."

"Not your place exactly," said Lafe. "Just here in the settlement. But I've been through it before I came to your place, my girl, an' Black ain't anywhere around. So I figured, with Rip bein' with him an all, maybe they'd finished up here."

Rip spoke quickly. "I didn't know we were supposed to come here an' meet you. But when Black ran out on me I figured he might come here an' hide out with the money . . . "

"He wouldn't hide out with me," put in Annie vehemently, raising her hand, revealing her delectable breast once more. "I never cottoned to the man."

"No, I guess he kept runnin'," said Rip.

Lafe said, "He wouldn't do that. He wouldn't let Dragoman down. Hell, they're brothers — even if they did pick different names for alias purposes."

"They're just half-brothers," said Rip. "Black tol' me that hisself." He chuckled sardonically. "It was one of the few things he did tell me, likely."

"You better tell me exactly what you reckoned happened," said Lafe, and he was being a mite sardonic now.

"You look kind of uncomfortable standing there, pardner," said Rip. He jerked his head forward. "There's another chair there. Why'n't you sit down?"

Lafe looked at the other chair which was only a few long steps away from him. And he had long legs. He crossed the space and lowered himself to the wooden seat of the chair and, for a breath of a moment, he took his eyes off the other man on his chair, and the girl in the bed.

Rip made his desperate move. And Annie screamed shrilly.

9

IT had been said that no man in his right mind would take cattle through the badlands. But Starke Dragoman was trying it and seemed to be succeeding. He had started another stampede — and maybe that had never been tried before.

He lost beef. That was inevitable. The corpses would lie rotting in the sun. There was little shelter over this barren waste which wasn't even a favourite haunt of predators, though the vultures began to hover in the metallic skies now, descending from time to time to the back of the herd, to squabble over fallen or limping animals.

Dragoman had calculated all this beforehand, however. He had expected to lose beef. He told his men not to waste their time or their bullets on the predators.

The ambush at the pass, then the landslide, had been a great success. The two marksmen who had engineered this plan had caught up with the rest and their reports had been good. But Dragoman still didn't take things for granted.

The whole plan — or *two* plans — had been well engineered and no small mistakes must be allowed to mar things now. Although it seemed unlikely, there might still be followers, and the echoes of gunfire could carry a long way in these desolate places.

A lone cat had followed the herd for a while after it had hit the badlands, but it soon gave up and returned to its haunts in the hills and the trees.

It was still a big herd, travelling more slowly now, when it hit the end of the badlands. "Keep 'em moving," Starke Dragoman shouted. "Keep 'em moving."

The cattle had spent themselves. There would be no more stampedes. But they were after water and sustenance now and they plodded steadily onwards like a slow, sluggish brown sea. Maybe the stupid beasts had some kind of sixth sense after all. They were nearing the end of their long, tiring, thirsty journey.

Dragoman had a good, well-trained bunch of outlaws, none of whom had come to any harm as yet. They did as he told them because he was the brain among them and was straightforward and pitiless. They knew his name was an alias, and he wasn't the only one among them who carried a label to which he didn't lawfully belong. They didn't know why Dragoman had picked such a high-falutin' moniker, but it seemed to suit him.

He was the eldest among them and it was fairly unlikely that any of them had heard of Obe Starke and Al Dragoman who, had they lived, would be real mossyhorns now. They had lasted well but had both gotten their come-uppance, and at the same time also, swinging from neighbouring trees.

The younker called Renfew had been with them earlier that day, for it was Starke and Dragoman who had taught him his nefarious trade.

The three of them had held up a stage coach, killed the driver and the shot-gun guard and taken a payroll bundle, robbing the passengers as well.

By the time the posse was on their heels they had done a share-out. Starke's horse had stumbled in a gopher-hole or something and thrown his rider badly, damaging his head and breaking his leg, the beast's too, which had had to be shot.

Dragoman wouldn't leave his partner, told young Renfew to go on alone. Renfew learned later that Dragoman had put up a good fight beside his half-conscious old pardner, who had tried to use a hand-gun. But the posse, little more than a bunch of bloodthirsty vigilantes, had hanged them both.

Renfew didn't know whether the avengers knew his name also — Starke and Dragoman had been notorious in their day — and would be after him, the law also, dodgers in law offices and the like, a price on his head. He rode hard and he rode long and he decided to change his name. He'd been an orphan on a crooked trail when the two veteran outlaws had picked him up. He owed them a lot. He repaid them by taking their names.

He decided eventually that nobody was after a younker called Renfew — and the new name Starke Dragoman would confuse anybody. That pleased the young man's growing, quirky humour. The two old-timers who had carried those monikers, whether their originals or not, being dead and buried. Forgotten too, except by pulp historians who were trying to make 'folk heroes' of such as they.

Renfew-Dragoman met his half-brother — they had once lived together on a dirt-farm — quite by chance. The half-brother, a little younger than Dragoman, was named Green. Dragoman was delighted to learn that the man, an owlhooter himself now, had changed his name to 'Black'; just Black. They teamed up and got a bunch together.

Now Dragoman, almost at the end of the journey with the stolen cattle, was beginning to wonder what had happened to Black, and to his partner, young Rip, and to Lafe whom he had sent to meet up with them. Although they would be coming by a different route they would be coming a lot faster than the herd now that the stampede was finished and should've caught up with them by now.

* * *

Mayor Mobane of Commoddee had had a wondering time all the way along on the last few days. He'd thought that if the Dakell herd had arrived on the range outside a day earlier the rustling and robbery would still have taken place. The drive had been a day late. Had that day been an extra chance for the folk who'd stolen the cattle, for the folk who'd stolen the money and killed the Dakell foreman, Tod Millen?

Who had known about the coming drive, the money? Had the news spread while that one odd day did also?

Were the robbery and the rustling part and parcel of one master plan or was this a terrible coincidence — and that seemed to old salesman Mobane, a student of men and matters and happenings, to be fairly unlikely.

He figured that Max Hardisty thought the same way. The tall marshal hadn't actually said so — but he seldom said anything unless he was sure, and then not too much. And Max's girl-friend, Nita, who had been with him when they first met up with Mobane, didn't seem to have any theory at all. And now was the funeral of the well-liked young man Tod, who had met his death in a room of Miss Nita's Superbe Hotel.

It was a big turn-out but a quiet one and soon over.

And the town waited for the return of its marshal and his sidekicks, Jed Spokes and Aldo Boner, the latter a Dakell man, the other foreman of Rancher Smithon's spread, the Twisted Spur.

Speculation grew, grief, fear . . .

10

LAFE was on the chair and was facing the other man — and the girl in the bed. His gun was still in his hand, but not so well lifted, not so well levelled as it had been. For one infinitesimal moment his concentration was not as it had been. And Rip moved. And Annie screamed.

Maybe the girl's scream threw Lafe more off balance than anything else. Annie just wasn't the screaming kind: the bitch had done it purposely!

Rip was almost upon him when Lafe fired the gun. His aim was too low. At close quarters the bullet smashed through Rip's thigh, destroying flesh and sinew and bone. But Rip's momentum carried him on and his clawing fingers clutched Lafe's throat.

Lafe went over backwards, taking the chair too, with a crash, a splintering sound. His gun skidded across the floor, almost joining Rip's belt and armoury where it lay.

Annic came out of the bed, naked, and grabbed the gun, turned towards the two struggling men, levelled the weapon. She did not then pull the trigger but remained poised. Rip was on top of Lafe and the splintered chair was under them, and sort of around them. Lafe was trying to force Rip's hands from his throat and both men were grunting mightily and they were both marred with blood: it didn't seem possible that there would be so much blood so soon.

Rip was losing a lot of blood but fury carried him on. He had a job to finish. Lafe's eyes were bulging, his face darkening, his mouth shooting open, showing his tongue and his feral-looking teeth. Rip's weight held him down. The chair splintered beneath him. It flattened out, debris under their combined weight. Lafe's arms seemed to be pinned.

His thrashings seemed to have no effect on the man who pinned him down, who slowly, powerfully, throttled him.

Rip's back muscles rippled in his lean, wiry frame, and Lafe began to choke, a horrible sound.

Annie lowered the gun, stood transfixed, aghast, her eyes staring in horror.

Lafe gave one last horrible gasp and lay still with Rip sprawled atop of him.

Annie went forward then, after placing the gun on the floor. She got down on one knee and reached out, and her nakedness became smeared with blood. "Rip," she said. "Rip." She feared he was dead too.

But then he began to gasp as he tried to rise, the effort making his shattered thigh pump blood more quickly than ever. Annie knew that if this wasn't stopped soon he would be finished just as surely as Lafe was.

She tried to help him. She was a

strong girl, but he was a dead weight. She became dappled with blood. She began to feel nauseous. Her head began to swim. She fought the feeling, trying to drag Rip across to the bed.

Miraculously, he was helping himself. Between them, they made it. He collapsed across the bed. She lifted his legs on to the top. They were like lead weights, the wounded one not pumping blood quite so much in his now-position but running red each side of the shattered member and staining the sheets.

In desperation Annie tore at cleaner sheets on the other side of the bed. Her anxiety gave her strength. She hadn't glanced once at the dead man at the back of her now.

She tore strips of white cloth and with this she tried to staunch the blood and form some kind of tourniquet. The leg looked very bad, a jagged hole appearing in the muscular fullness of the young man's thigh as the blood was mopped up, staunched somewhat — but not enough — ejecting in sluggish spurts.

There was a deathly silence now. Annie heard the front door open, then footsteps. A tall gangling man with iron-grey hair appeared in the bedroom doorway. In his hand he held a long-barrelled Dragoon Colt. There was a long cheroot in his mouth.

"I heard a shot. Annie, what . . . ?"

"Help me, Ceegar. Please help me."

★ ★ ★

"Yeh, I know the settlement," Jed Spokes said. "It used to be famous for a kind of gamblin' hell visited by different folk. I don't think it's there now."

"Notorious was the word for it," said Marshal Max Hardisty. "And it's still there. Part of it anyhow. Old Ceegar ain't as young as he used to be and has curtailed his activities somewhat. He still has the big card games there from time to time an' quite legitimate bettors come from far an' wide for them."

"It was an owlhoot roost."

"It still is, partly, I guess. But as long as the owl-hooters don't bother Ceegar, he don't bother them. Once a bunch tried to stick up a big game an' met some pretty rough retaliation. One of 'em was killed. The others high-tailed. Ceegar's got some good gunnies watching out for him."

"That stick-up, I heard about that," said young Aldo Boner.

"Yeh?" Hardisty wondered how Aldo, who came from miles away from this territory and was only sort of visiting now, had got to hear about the failed robbery.

Still, Hardisty knew Aldo's boss, Bill Dakell, from way back, a straight man and a fine rancher. And Bill had recommended Aldo, had even said the young ranny was pretty good with a gun.

Hardisty had noted that Aldo wore soft leather riding gloves. Maybe he used these too, when doing his ranching chores, and the hands beneath them weren't horny ranny's hands but supple and fast.

"Why do they call that old-time gambler 'Ceegar'?" Aldo wanted to know.

Hardisty said, "He's allus smoked all kinds of cigars. Big ceegars mostly. An' long and black. Ceegars that might choke another man." The tall man split one of his rare grins, white, even teeth gleaming in brown face.

"As far's I can remember he's never been known by anything else but that nickname. It's sort of 'is trademark. He's noted for square dealin' an' all. You're straight with Ceegar an' he won't mess with you."

"That's a fact I guess," said Jed Spokes.

"You think that runaway killer might be in Ceegar's town then?" Aldo asked.

"I dunno," said Hardisty. "Pays to look in there, though. Might pick up some information anyway."

They quit talking, till the marshal said, "We'll go round the other way." And he wheeled his horse.

11

IT was mainly clapboard, with 'dobe foundation, but it was on two floors. It was the only two-storey building in the settlement which had in fact mostly been referred to as Ceegar's Place by regulars. Even though it had a neighbouring creek there wasn't much doing in the barren lands around, which were so close to the actual badlands.

The gambling fraternity gathered here, and the outlaws came and went, shifty, watchful-eyed. They watched the creek side of the settlement most of all, for folks were more likely to come from that direction: the other side faced out towards the badlands and, beyond them, the border between New Mexico — where Ceegar's Place stood — and Texas.

Texas law or Texas bounty hunters were hardly likely to cross the badlands in search of quarry or dodger-evaders, unless they had burrs in their asses or great vengeance in their hearts.

The young wounded outlaw called Rip was carried by some of Ceegar's boys to the saloon which was also part of the so-called Gambling Hell and was the only really good drinking place in the settlement, though hooch could be got in other holes in the wall.

The boy was placed on a long cleared table with a cushion under his head. There was no doctor hereabouts but Ceegar had rudimentary medical knowledge and he got to work. He knew Rip slightly but had no great feelings about him either one way or the other. But Rip was Annie's friend and Ceegar treated Annie like the daughter he'd never had. He, in fact, had no living family as far as he knew. Annie, although she had her own little business, was Ceegar's dealer and sometimes roulette-wheel jockey when the place was busy.

The body of the outlaw called Lafe

had been placed in a disused barn and would be buried at some later time.

Rip was totally unconscious. Ceegar worked on him, following the procedures that Annie had begun. The wounded leg was a shrouded mess of blood.

"He's lost too much blood," said the tall, gangling man with the iron-grey hair. "He needs a transfusion."

"What's a transfusion, boss?" asked one of the young bully boys.

"More blood, you idiot," said Ceegar. "But we haven't got the facilities for a thing like that here. He needs a hospital, but he'd probably die before we could get him there. Get me a couple of blankets and two of those trestles we used to use when we needed more tables."

The cresfallen minion and one of his pards ran to get the necessary. Ceegar looked at Annie and said, "We'll take him up to bed."

★ ★ ★

The law trio had made a wide detour and they came in at the back of the settlement as the sun was waning and their long shadows, like the ghosts of horses and men, spread across the dust and the ruts ahead of them. There weren't many folks in this apology of a main street and nobody paid much heed to the newcomers. Drifters. They came, they went. Too much attention might be resented, even acted upon. Let 'em be!

They made for the tall building, slowed their horses. There was nobody on the stoop. They'd been a mite too late to spot the old-timer who'd been sitting on the wooden chair in the shade, but he had spotted them. He was now running up the stairs at the top of which he was accosted by one of Ceegar's boys.

"Three strangers," the old man panted. "Looks like they're comin' in."

"Go down. Watch 'em. I'll tell the boss."

The oldster did as he was told. The bully boy went along the passage and into the room where were the wounded outlaw, the girl, the boss. He passed on the news.

"They might be after this boy," Ceegar said. "Watch 'em. Tell two more of the boys. If they try to come up here, you stop 'em. But no shooting, y'understand."

"All right, boss."

* * *

The three men entered into the saloon part of the establishment and saw an old-timer watching them curiously. But most old-timers seemed to be nosy anyway.

Over at the long bar there were three other, younger men.

Aldo and Jed sat at a table and Hardisty walked towards the trio at the bar. There didn't seem to be a keep behind the bar.

Hardisty had a sort of negligent, almost

catlike walk. He asked laconically, "Open for business?"

"I can serve you, suh," said one of the young men and he went around behind the bar.

Hardisty ordered three whiskeys an' leave the bottle. While the voluntary barman served him the two other young men watched him.

But then, at a small jerk of the head from the tall customer his two companions left their table and strolled across the floor and joined him.

The barman rejoined his two companions.

The members of the two trios stole surreptitious glances at each other. The nosy old-timer sidled up to the bar.

"Get your own, Jigger," said the erstwhile barman curtly.

The old man moved behind the bar and rattled bottles and glasses. "Anybody else want anything now?" he wheedled. He seemed all eyes and ears.

"Take your booze an' take your leave, Jigger," said another of the three bully boys. "Get out of here."

A bottle under one arm and a glass in the other hand, the oldster scuttled away, disappeared.

"Nosy old bastard," said the third bully boy.

Nobody argued with him about that.

The big room was now empty except for the half-dozen men.

It was the tall stranger who spoke now. A mite older than all the others but still a young man. Lean face, dark hair, a loose look about him as if he didn't give a damn for anything or anybody. Definitely a man to watch, though, as he looked slowly but without any offence about him at the three keepers of the house.

"Ceegar still around?" he asked.

"He's upstairs," said one of the men, and the other two looked hard at him as if he'd spoken out of turn.

But then the one who might have been classed as 'the barman' seemed to take the initiative, asking, "You know Ceegar, mister?"

"Used to." Laconic as all hell.

And the tall man's two younger companions watching everybody with lively interest.

And now their leader — and he was so obviously the leader — became less laconic, took the initiative out of everybody's hand, turning on his heels, saying, "I'll go upstairs an' find Ceegar."

"You ain't allowed up there, mister," said the barman and he reached for the pistol at the holster in his belt. But Aldo Boner was quicker than him, backing, a gun in his hand as if by a twist of magic.

The barman's weapon was not pulled: he'd let it slide back out of harm's way. His two companions had been taken aback.

"Don't none o' you boys try anything now," Aldo told them. "Up the hands a bit. Up 'em."

They 'upped' 'em.

The tall man turned. His movements were almost negligent, or studiously so, as he put his hand in the pocket of his scuffed hide vest and brought forth a shining star and pinned it to his breast. "Don't mess with my two deputies, boys," he said.

Jed Spokes, standing beside Aldo, had his gun out now also, and he said, "This is Marshal Hardisty of Commoddee."

One of the bully boys — not the barman, who still had his mouth open — exclaimed, "I thought . . . I thought . . . Yeh, Hardisty, Hardisty . . . " But then the younker was gazing past the man with the star, and the barman had shut his mouth; and the third bully boy was looking almost lively.

And a voice behind Hardisty said, "Drop that Colt, whelp, or your tall friend gets a load o' buckshot in his spine."

Aldo dropped his weapon. The five boys were pretty close there at the bar. A shot-gun blast would've scattered them, friend and foe, but Hardisty would've gotten the worse of it. So half-a-dozen men froze like so many statues.

There was a split moment of silence. Then, though Hardisty's voice was soft, deep, it rang out, making eyes start.

"I know that voice, and I know its owner can handle a shot-gun like it was his third arm. I'm raising my mitts and I'm going to turn around slowly."

"That you, Max Hardisty?" said the other voice.

"Hello, Ceegar." Then the tall man was all the way round and facing the other tall, older man with the iron-grey hair and the long cheroot smoking in his mouth. And the double-barrel in his fists slowly lowering, behind him the oldster called Jigger, without his bottle now.

"How've you been, Max?"

"Tol'able, Ceegar. Tol'able. You?"

"Yeh, tol'able." The old man, shot-gun grounded now, gave a little spurt of laughter. "To what do we owe the honour of this visit?"

"I'm lookin' for somebody."

"I figured . . . " Ceegar let the sentence tail off.

"These boys are my deputies." Hardisty jerked his lean, dark head in its battered light-brown Stetson.

"The other boys are my boys, they were just trying to protect me."

"I know. They did pretty good I guess."

"Yeh." Ceegar looked past Hardisty, went on, "You can leave us now, my pretties. Marshal Hardisty is an old friend."

Heads lowered, the three bully boys filed out. "Come with me, Max," Ceegar said.

Hardisty made a gesture to his deputies, signalling them to stay put. Jigger shuffled over to them, obviously keen on replacing the bottle that his boss had doubtless taken from him. Ceegar let him go. The two tall men passed through the door, disappeared from the sight of the two young men and the oldster at the bar as Aldo, his gun long since pouched, grinned at Jigger.

12

IT had been a hard drive, a stampede across cattle country, then the hills and the pass, and finally the badlands. But the herd was watering now, and it was still a big herd.

On the last lap of the long trail the rustlers eased the beeves along, and presently riders came forward from the borderlands to help them, and then they all saw the ranch buildings, the rolling green all around. And they were still on the New Mexico side of the border, which surprised some of them.

But this had been a daring plan all along, hadn't it?

Pursuers, if there were still any of these — and that hardly seemed likely right now — would expect the herd to be taken over the border to the Texas cattlelands not to this lonely place on the same side of the border and still under New Mexico Jurisdiction.

But cattle could be just as easily mingled here brands changed, with smaller herds from various sources, driven, sold elsewhere, Twisted Spur beef mingled with the rest, disappearing piecemeal with other stock.

Starke Dragoman met up with the owner of the ranch and they seemed to know each other well. But there was still a worry in Dragoman's dark eyes in the lantern-jawed face with the crooked scar on the left temple, white in the brown sun-blistered tight flesh. There was a *tightness* about Starke's whole demeanour and those of his men who knew him and his plans — part of 'em anyway — knew what was bothering him.

Black, Rip and Lafe had not returned. Was there a doublecross? Could Dragoman's half-brother, Black, be guilty of such a thing? Or was that wild boy guilty? The wild boy called

111

Rip! And what had happened to the pale killer called Lafe who had gone looking for the two partners who had the cattle money, the extra gold topping that had made this latest job, the best ever, the richest? Had three men come to grief? Where was the money now?

Dragoman's men walked around him as if he was surrounded by eggs. His scar writhed; his face was devilish . . .

Dragoman had other problems, though, that his men didn't know about. Problems with the buyer of the stolen cattle, the man whose greed for land and stock had sparked off at least half of the caper that, it seemed, wasn't quite finished after all only Dragoman knew how actually half-finished it was. And the half-knowledge was eating at his guts.

The two boss-men had done business together before and there'd always been a haggle. Dragoman expected a haggle. It was all part of the way the two of them, ruthless, powerful, single-minded to the point of madness, did business.

His name was Silas Boyard and he was bigger than Dragoman in every way, something which deep in his black heart the outlaw leader bitterly resented. He was even bigger in stature than Dragoman, and Dragoman was not a small man. But Boyard was six foot four and had no adipose on him at all, was a bit older than Dragoman but didn't look it. He was emperor of all he surveyed and further — and he looked and acted the part. He was an arrogant man with flowing yellow hair and a wide moustache and he played the *grandee* as wholeheartedly as any Mexican-Spanish *don* on the far borderlands on the other side of Texas.

Dragoman had to always see him alone in his grand wood-panelled study but there were always two of Boyard's *pistoleros* in attendance and, despite his own arrogance, the outlaw leader felt intimidated.

Not this time, though, for Dragoman had uncertainties on his mind and this made him peevish and, as his followers knew, when he was peevish he was kind of lethal also. But Boyard didn't know this, or didn't care anyway.

Dragoman had to think fast.

He said, "There's somep'n I haven't told you."

"What's that?"

"I have some horses as well. Leastways, I'm expecting some horses. A horse ranch we came across. Not a big one but some prime stock. Some o' my boys took it. Some killin', some drivin', no problem."

"How many head?"

"About twenty I guess."

"That isn't a lot."

"Prime stock I said. The two oldsters who ran the place have been in the business for a long time. If they don't know their horseflesh nobody does."

"Where are these horses?"

"Haven't arrived yet. Those boys had to catch up."

It was all lies, of course. There hadn't been a horse ranch near the trail, not as far as Dragoman knew anyway. And, if there had been, he wouldn't have stopped the rush of the herd once they were going good, wouldn't have stopped the boys. With Black, Rip and Lafe mysteriously still missing — unless they'd turned up while he was talking to Boyard — he couldn't afford to let any more go a-roving.

He rose, said, "I'll go check. Mebbe those horses are here by now. Mebbe we can do a better deal — with the horses an' all."

"Yeh," said Boyard non-committally.

Dragoman had been taking things in. Surreptitious, darting glances — way he felt now, didn't care whether Boyard noticed 'em or not . . . Shifty himself, getting shiftier. Double-dealing bastard. Treacherous and dangerous. Mighty dangerous.

The safe was there behind Boyard. A big heavy safe with a sort of ship's-wheel on the front of it. Dragoman had, of course seen the safe on other occasions, seen Boyard open it, his back to the visitor.

And the two *pistoleros*, not always the same two but always two. One outside the door, unseen by Dragoman or the man's boss. The other outside the window to the left of the visitor in the visitor's chair on the opposite side of the desk to the boss. Watching. Dragoman could sense him watching now.

Going out he passed the boy outside the door, who gave him a negative glance from cold eyes. Me an' the boys have walked into a killers' nest, Dragoman suddenly thought. Maybe Boyard had been waiting all along for the big grab. And the herd that the rustler chief and his boys had brought along this time was the biggest ever.

Dragoman couldn't spot his boys right off but figured they were in the bunkhouse playing poker with some of the ranch hands who were on their time off. This was pretty usual. His boys had friends among the ranch hands who had no reason to mistrust them or their leader.

Dragoman looked back. The one young *pistolero* was still outside the boss's window. The other one hadn't come outside on to the porch. Maybe he was Boyard's regular bodyguard or something.

Dragoman found his boys, called them out. He spoke fast. There was no argument, just a few questions. These boys were still ready for any kind of devilry. They split up. Dragoman went back to Boyard.

Dragoman told the ranch-boss that the boys with the horses hadn't turned up yet and he was worried that something might have happened to them, even that a posse was after them. He said he didn't want any posse to arrive at Boyard's place. Boyard said, goddammit, no. Dragoman said he figured him and the men he'd got here should go out looking for those boys, horses or not, posse or not.

"Maybe if somep'n happened that

I didn't plan, we mightn't be able to come back. So I'll take the offer for the cattle for the time being. All right?"

"All right," said Boyard and he got up from his chair and turned towards the safe.

13

"**W**HERE'D you put the money, son?" asked Hardisty. The grey sweat-bedewed face looked up at him. The young eyes were cloudy but there was still a defiant light in their depths.

The boy called Rip said, "I don't know anything about any money, or any robbery or anything. I didn't come here with a partner either. I was by myself."

Hardisty had already ascertained that this latter part was the truth. But he didn't believe any of the rest of it. Furthermore, the oldster called Jigger who worked for Ceegar had been outside when he first saw the young stranger and he had seen the latter take saddle-bags from his saddle and carry them into Annie's cabin.

When Hardisty had first looked at

Rip, the young hardcase had been unconscious, but he wasn't that now and the Commoddee marshal wanted some answers. A robbery had been committed back in his town and a man had been killed: Bill Dakell's foreman, Tod Millen, a man not much older than the one in the bed, a man Hardisty had known and liked.

Hardisty had had a chance to talk to Annie, whom he knew from way back before Rip's time, had known far better than anybody here realized, except maybe that veteran reprobate called Ceegar.

Annie said she hadn't been at home when Rip arrived and she hadn't seen any saddle-bags. They'd looked in her place. The bedroom was a mess. A man had died in there and another had bled plentifully. But it didn't look as if anything had been hidden there. Or in the kitchen, the sitting-room, the outhouse and privy.

Hardisty had taken a look at the man who'd been throttled by the wounded

Rip. A man called Lafe whom Annie knew as a friend of Rip's, though he certainly hadn't acted as a friend, not right then.

Hardisty had recognized Lafe as an owlhooter, thought he might have a dodger on the man back in his office. Annie had said that she thought both Rip and Lafe had been involved with a man called Starke Dragoman. Such a funny name, it had stuck in her mind. Hardisty had heard the name before, he thought, hadn't met the gent though, didn't know anything about him.

The marshal was kind of peeved about that.

The marshal remembered a dead man tied to a horse back on the trail. The trail he and his boys had followed. The wrong trail. A rattlesnake-bitten corpse, a horse and saddle, nothing else.

The marshal had taken a look at Rip's horse, still browsing contentedly outside Annie's place. There were signs the cayuse had been ridden hard, though.

He also had more accoutrements on him than were needed, accoutrements that could have belonged to another horse, another rider, everything double except for a saddle. His rider it seemed had even toted two rifles, one of which was in Annie's cabin, the other in the lean-to where the corpse of the strangled Lafe had been laid . . .

Rip had subsided again, closed his eyes. He looked awful. It was hard to tell whether he'd passed out again or was just playing possum. He was a mighty sick boy, though, and that was for sure.

Hardisty didn't know whether Rip was going to make it. He had Rip labelled as a killer. A coward who'd shoot an unarmed man through a door. Whether it was Rip's bullet that had killed Tod Millen, or his partner's bullet, was a moot point and not worth a damn. Hardisty would have preferred to take Rip back to Commoddee for justice . . . But if Rip was about to cash in his chips right here, what the hell!

But Hardisty wanted answers first and he wanted them as fast as possible.

Rip had lost too much blood. He needed more pumped into him. But where could he get this — and how? Hardisty looked down at the still form and felt a blinding sense of frustration.

Annie had come back with him. And Ceegar was there too.

Hardisty turned to the girl. "We'll go back to your place," he said. "And this time we'll look good, real good."

It was like a curt command.

"All right, Max," the dark-haired girl said meekly.

Hardisty looked at Ceegar, jerked his thumb sideways in the direction of the bed. "If this one comes to his senses will you send one of my boys to tell me?"

"I will, pardner."

Dragoman? Well, Hardisty had gotten a name at least. Had Dragoman in some way been behind the rustling? And in some way the robbery too? Anyway, where were the cattle?

That would have to wait though, that was just meat on the hoof. Big; maybe not so hard to find eventually. The money was the main thing right now, Hardisty figured. The need to get hold of it was like bile in his guts. He hastened his steps, wobbling a bit on his high-heeled riding boots, Annie in her moccasins trotting at his side.

★ ★ ★

Dragoman glanced towards the window. The young *pistolero* was no longer there.

There was a thump against the door. That was careless, thought Dragoman.

Boyard turned halfway away from the safe which he already had open.

"What was that?" he said.

"Stay right as you are, friend," said Dragoman and he rose with his gun in his hand.

Boyard's head was twisted. He wasn't in a good position. "What . . . ?" he began, his voice rising.

"Quiet," chided Dragoman. "And easy."

The gun pointed at the man who stood awkwardly frozen, Dragoman moved around the desk. "Move over to the side so as I can see what you're doing. And then empty the safe, putting everything on the desk. I know you keep a shooter in the desk drawer. I just want to make sure you ain't got one in the safe as well."

"What'll you do if I tell you to go to hell?" Boyard asked.

"I'll kill you an' empty the safe myself."

"One shot an' my boys will come in," said Boyard.

"Your two bodyguard boys ain't able to come in any more. And the rest would be too late I guess."

Suddenly Boyard looked uncertain. He could see the window, no man behind it. And there had been a thump outside the door.

Boyard moved sideways. "I'll get you later, damn your hide," he said.

"Don't count on it."

Boyard began to empty the safe. There was no weapon in there, but there was plenty of valuable stuff. Greenbacks, packages which obviously contained gold coin. Deeds and things like that which were of no importance to the man with the gun who didn't move an inch but called, "Come in, Rab."

The door opened and a stocky feller came in with a gunny sack, grinned at his leader, crossed to the desk and began to fill the sack, sweeping odd documents and envelopes on to the floor as he did so.

Dragoman moved nearer to Boyard as the safe emptied, as the gunny sack began to bulge.

With a quick sleight of hand Dragoman swapped right for left. Then he used his right hand to bring forth a broad-bladed wicked-looking knife from a pouch behind his belt.

He moved behind Boyard, who tried

to turn but wasn't quick enough as the knife was raised, slashed sideways across his throat, sweeping deeply and creating a wide red mouth from which blood spurted.

Without a sound, Boyard fell forward across the desk and on top of the papers and envelopes that hadn't been swept to the floor.

The body slid from there, leaving smears of blood on crumpled paper and polished wood and Dragoman stepped back as the man with the bulging gunny sack watched in horrified interest, his eyes glinting.

The body slumped to the floor on its face. Dragoman bent down and wiped the blade of his knife on Boyard's clean linsey shirt at the back. He returned the weapon to his belt and his other weapon, the Navy Colt, to its holster.

"All right, move," he said.

The bodyguard lay curled up on his side in the passage.

"You were kinda noisy, Rab," said Dragoman.

"I guess. I stuck my gun in his back an' the cheeky bastard turned on me, an' he was fast, I tell yuh, chief. I slugged him hard though . . . "

"You certainly did." Dragoman was bending, peering. He chuckled evilly. "You must've lost your temper all right. You caved his head in. He's mutton . . . Let's go check out back."

"Dilly," said Rab. "He'd use his knife. With a knife he's almost as good as you are."

The tubby, squint-eyed Dilly didn't look fast but obviously was. The second bodyguard had gone the way of his partner, one knife-wound in the back, another deeply in the front, probably right into the heart.

"I told the rest of the boys to be by the corral," said Dragoman.

There'd been no shooting, no undue noise of any kind. Nobody got in their way. One of the cowboys even waved a hand, taking them as leaving, wishing them well.

Those boys knew their boss bought

cattle without questioning where it came from. As long as they were good hands, tight-mouthed, they knew they were settled. They weren't dumb enough, or curious enough, to be questioning anything.

The herd was being watched over and desultorily counted by three men. Luckily, they were pretty close together and the Dragoman boys had them covered, guns bristling, before they could open their mouths. Then one of them asked, "What's goin' on?" A hard-bitten, middle-aged cuss with scraggly red hair shot with grey.

"We'll take over here again, Raithe," said Dragoman. "Take your gunbelts off, very easy now."

"You're askin' for all hell, Dragoman," said the grizzled Raithe, the eldest of the trio and obviously their leader.

"Do as you're told, or I'll shoot you outa the saddle."

The gunbelts thudded to the ground and, at a signal from Dragoman, one of his boys dismounted, gathered up the hardware and draped it over his saddle.

"Walk," said Dragoman.

Raithe was speechless now. He gave the outlaw leader one more look of pure hate and then he led the other two men towards the ranch buildings.

The outlaws were all mounted again, some with the reins of spare horses in their fists. The three riderless mounts weren't to be allowed to follow their masters, who were trotting awkwardly now.

Dragoman said, "I want the herd stampeded like before an' right at the ranch. Most of 'em seem to be aimin' that way." He gave his burbling laugh as the boys looked at him. He drew his gun and fired two rapid shots into the air.

The boys, like performing monkeys, followed their leader's example, blasting the air, screaming and yippeeing.

The horses reared. They had a job to hold the riderless ones. The cattle moved in thunder and in dust, their pace quickly growing in momentum.

Two of the horses broke loose. "Let 'em go," yelled Dragoman. Their owners couldn't be seen now, were hidden by the swirling dust. The riderless horses went off at a tangent, scared witless by the moiling, moving mass of beef. There were small gaps. And a man yelled, "I saw that redheaded man go down."

"Looked like it," bawled another man. "I can't see the other two, though."

The dust swirled back at the riders as they coughed and spluttered, not shouting any more then. Pulling their bandannas up over their mouths and noses while trying to hold their fractious mounts who wanted to be away with their fellows, in any direction as long as it was away from this noisy, bewildering shennanigan.

This was their second stampede, which they didn't fancy any more than they'd fancied the other one. But the dust was swirling away on all sides and the rustlers saw the cattle hit the ranch-buildings, saw men running in all directions, saw buildings falling but didn't hear them because of the roar of the frantic herd; and it was all like a dream, a nightmare.

But not *their* nightmare.

Dragoman was well content. He didn't need the cattle. Didn't want 'em. Had been paid for 'em. Had taken his pay for them — in spades. And then some! Plenty more for him and his men. And even those who hadn't understood his sudden action, throwing the cattle away it seemed, would eventually be well pleased.

But there was the money that had been taken at the town called Commoddee. At least, he hoped it had been taken, hoped nothing had gone terribly wrong. He had to find out what had happened. He had to find Black and Rip — and Lafe.

He turned his horse about. He swung an arm. "Let's go," he shouted.

14

HARDISTY had known Annie before, just as he had known Ceegar and others of the older, more settled of the denizens of the isolated settlement.

Annie picked her men and, years ago, she'd picked Hardisty. And he had allowed himself to be picked, he who usually did the picking himself and had been described by acquaintances as a killer with the fillies, a devil for all seasons with the female population, had been described in far less complimentary terms by fellers whose women had turned to the tall man with blue eyes who always seemed to come out of the sun on a prime horse.

But that had been in his younger days, he told himself, ignoring the fact that he was still a young man, though not exactly an infant prodigy.

But he was more kind of responsible, he thought, being a marshal and all. And then there was Nita back in Commoddee: Nita and he had been through some fine times together before they both settled down.[1]

Settled down! That was a questionable thing. Hell, he was on the trail again like any hired gun — which was what he was after all, always had been.

A quieter time right now, however, an investigating time with Annie in her cabin on the edge of the settlement.

Had circumstances been different, after his meeting up with Annie again after a long time, they might have taken up where they left off. Hardisty had a feeling about this . . .

Still and all, he couldn't quite understand why Annie had taken up with a young killer like Rip. But that she had done it seemed. Periodically,

[1] See *The Trail Rats*

there seemed an almost shy restraint in her manner towards her old lover. Hardisty knew he could overcome this if he tried. But this wasn't the time, not even the place. Definitely not the place, this still bloodstained scene. For he was in the bedroom now, leaving the girl in the bigger room behind him. And he was searching.

He was a detective and he knew the secret places. Women weren't the only folk who had their secret places . . .

He bent and probed and knocked and stamped. He opened and shut doors and moved things around. He took the room by sections, starting, naturally, at the door. He found nothing. He went to the window last and looked out at the flatlands and the sun glinting on the sparse waters of the narrow creek.

Nothing moved out there and there was a silence. Until Hardisty began to drum with his feet. Then he bent and took out his jack-knife and clicked out the blade with his thumb.

He heard the door open in the

other room and a man's voice, the girl answering it. He returned the knife to its place and straightened and crossed the room and passed through the communicating door.

Aldo Boner was facing Annie, saw his chief over her shoulder, said, "Rip's opened his eyes. He's bad though, an' Ceegar says for you to come right away, Marshal. Rip's cryin' an' complainin' and ain't making much sense. He's like a baby, an' weak."

"I'll come."

"I'll come with you," said Annie.

★ ★ ★

Raithe was coughing, the sounds bursting from his chest like gunshots, rocking his head. His vision was hazy. He didn't know whether this was due to the dust or to hurts he'd sustained from the stampeding cattle and the hard ground. He hoped he wasn't hurt badly but was scared he might be. He had seemed to be in the midst of — no, underneath! — stampeding hooves and frenzied bodies.

He crouched down as a few stragglers went past him. He was still alive, should thank his lucky stars for that.

Goddamn you, he cursed himself, you've been hurt before, stir yourself for Chrissakes!

The dust seemed to be clearing — or maybe his vision was getting better, though his head thudded like a mining hammer driving into hard rock. Running brown asses — that was all he could see.

He raised himself on his elbows, then had to pause as another spate of coughing tore at him, punching his chest, banging his head. But he struggled upwards to his knees. Then he had to rest. Were there more cattle? He tried to look behind, but then a wave of nausea hit him and he couldn't see a thing. But ahead of him there was a lot of noise: it was all part of the sounds that were punishing him.

He made a superhuman effort, rising

in a great rush, the whole of his body complaining. But then he was on his feet, swaying, getting his balance, managing to stay upright. Then he began to walk.

He looked straight ahead, fearing that if he looked at the ground it would come up and hit him. He limped, throwing himself sideways. Warm blood trickled from his temple and down the side of his face. Peevishly he wiped it off with his sleeve. Both his arms seemed to be functioning all right.

He stumbled over something, almost fell. He was forced to look down then.

It was one of the two boys who'd been with him when the Dragoman gang jumped them and stampeded the herd. It had been a great surprise. And what he looked down at now was pure horror.

The cowboy had been stamped into the earth by many sharp hooves and was only a mass of blood and bone, tattered flesh and pulped clothing, the body on its face, Raithe only able to identify it by fragments of cloth from the garish red, white and blue shirt the man had been wearing as a sort of tribute to his English ancestry. He had been a drifter who Raithe, as ranch foreman, had taken on, given a chance. He had been a good hand though, had answered to the name of Bart.

That could've been me, thought Raithe, swaying. In fact, he figured that he'd been nearer to the centre of the stampeding herd than this boy had, or his partner, wherever he was now.

Raithe staggered onwards. Then he saw the other boy, swaying in front of the wreckages of what had once been fine ranch-buildings and outhouses.

Raithe made a spurt. Carried on by his own momentum, he almost knocked the boy over when he reached him. They clung together. The boy, the youngest of the three of them, was gasping and whimpering. But he managed to get out, "Where's Bart?"

"He's dead, son, there's nothing

we can do for him but gather him together."

"Why . . . ?" Then the boy was lost for words.

"I don't know why, not rightly. But what's happened is bad, and we've got to find out how bad."

It proved to be worse than Raithe might have expected.

Men were running about like mutilated chickens. Others were just wandering in a dazed condition. Some were trying to do something about the wreckage and some of their pards who might be under that wreckage. Some, like Raithe, had had miraculous escapes. But there were others lying still on the beaten earth, others propped up awaiting help that nobody seemed to be able to give them yet. Somewhere a man called plaintively. There were other cries, muffled, as from a grave.

Some of the cattle could still be seen running but slowing down. Others had run their string, were browsing on the ground behind the ranch-buildings as if nothing had happened.

The front of the ranchhouse had been caved in. Through part of a window, glassless, leaning sideways, a man clambered out into the sun, his face blackened, his eyes wild. The Mexican cook far from his old borderland home on the other side of Texas. He had years ago crossed two borders to reach this post and keep to it well. Now he looked as if, though he hadn't lost his life, he had lost his senses.

"Miguel," Raithe called.

The dark head swivelled from side to side and finally the dark, mad-looking eyes fastened on the foreman and Miguel spoke his name.

Raithe started towards him and Miguel, who had faithfully served Rancher Boyard for many years, turned back towards the ruined house and gestured and began to make an eerie whining noise.

Holding on to himself, Raithe turned to look about him. He saw two men who looked dirty but unhurt, and he yelled at them. They ran across, one of them limping. They followed him into the wreckage of the house, while behind them, the cowboy who'd been involved with the herd stood stupidly looking at the Mexican cook who, himself unmoving also, kept on with his mindless lament.

15

"HE'S dead, Max," said Ceegar. "I've seen wounds like that before, during the war. He lost too much blood. Too much too fast. The life was drained from him."

"Did he say somep'n that you thought was interesting?"

"No-oo, not a thing, old friend. Not a thing. Made no sense at all. Pity to see such a younker die like that."

"He was a killer," said Hardisty flatly. "We'll bury him with his friend Lafe."

"Lafe killed him, and he killed Lafe. That makes 'em enemies I guess."

"I thought Lafe was Rip's friend," said Annie. "Yes, he was. I'd seen them together before. They were friends then."

"Friends become enemies sometimes," said Hardisty. "Particularly when money is involved. I remember Lafe from way back. I knew about him. A back-shooting owlhooter."

The two old friends and the girl (another 'old friend') were in the big room, standing by the bar just the three of them. Aldo Boner and Jed Spokes were in the place too, but they sat at a table in a corner with drinks in front of them. They were out of earshot of the others. Aldo had left a drink unfinished when he ran to fetch the marshal from Annie's place. None of Ceegar's boys were in the vicinity now.

Ceegar, puffing as usual at a pungent weed, went round the other side of the bar and poured drinks for his two friends and himself. Three hefty whiskies.

Hardisty looked over the top of his glass at Annie. "Tell me about all of it," he said.

"I guess I told you most."

"Tell me again. Tell me about all of it. The shootin' an' all. Try an' remember everything that was said."

"I don't remember much was said. It was all so bewildering. And it seemed to happen so quickly." Annie's handsome face was set, her dark blue eyes somewhat hooded.

Hardisty wondered, did she grieve for Rip? Was there something she didn't intend to tell him? Well, maybe that was understandable. But he was the investigator, the hunter . . .

Her voice was even, though, when she said, "I'll try to remember. Maybe more. I'll tell you all I can."

She left out the intimate details but forced herself to look up into Hardisty's blue eyes, paler than her own, eyes that were blisteringly direct, as piercing as dry ice to the skin. She could feel the blood rising in her face, warming her cheeks. She knew that this tall man who she had once known so well could divine so much, maybe more than she would have been prepared to tell him. But her thoughts were jumbled anyway, her feelings and memories terribly uncertain, her motives (if she had any) shrouded in shadows.

She wondered, did he blame her for anything?

No, she didn't think he did: he wasn't the kind.

She thought she couldn't tell him much more of significance than she'd already told him.

She stopped talking. She lowered her head. He was still looking at her. He said, "Yeh, Black who was mentioned must surely have been the body me an' the boys found, the sidewinder victim." He paused. Then he went on, "Let's go back to your place an' take up where we left off."

He began to move. And Ceegar, who seemed to be anticipating his tall old friend's every move said, "I'll look after things here, Max."

Unspeaking now, Annie followed Hardisty towards the door. Aldo and Jed both half-rose, looking towards their leader.

"Wait, boys," he said and they nodded, subsided again.

★ ★ ★

Foreman Raithe with his hard-bitten face and his thin, scrubby red hair shot with grey, well, he was the ramrod and, ultimately, he took over as he had to do. There was nothing he could do for his old saddle-pard, his boss, Silas Boyard, a battered corpse now, throat slit from ear to ear, as dead as a carved pig half-eaten by ravaging cannibals.

Raithe didn't stop for grieving or sorrowful words. He got his best boys together — those who hadn't already perished or weren't fit to ride — and he led them out. The terrible mess that remained of the great ranch could be cleared up by those who were left behind: they would do the best they could, as Raithe and his men would, trackers on a terrible vengeance trail.

The tracking was pretty easy, however. Raithe had it figured where Starke Dragoman and his gang were making for, and the signs were there and the redheaded foreman was proved right and the boys followed him as they'd always done.

"Those bastards," Raithe said. "They thought they could get away with anything. Now they think they're clearing the slate."

The boys were clean now and their horses were clean. They had taken time for that. They had provisions too, in case the trail took longer than Raithe hoped. And they had gathered enough armoury around them to start a war.

"Has Dragoman got friends where he's goin'?" one man wanted to know.

"Could be," said Raithe grimly. "But nothin' we can't handle I guess."

These weren't just horny-handed cowboys. Some of them were picked gunfighters: Boyard had always kept a crew like that. And all of them were proficient with a long gun as most cowboys were. Silas Boyard had been a foxey old bastard but he'd been a good boss to work for and they'd been his boys and owed him: killin' was what they had to do for him now, to do for his memory.

The man who led them could've told them a few tales about their late boss, if he figured he had the time to do so. He never had, and he sure as hell didn't have the time now. But he and Boyard had gone way, way back.

As hot-blooded younkers they rode the owlhoot trail together, and, like so many of their kind, cattle had been their targets. They'd been no better than Starke Dragoman and his gang, robbing and killing and burning and running out with as much stock as they could find, taking it from Arizona, New Mexico or Texas — they'd had a wide bailiwick and selling it to buyers on the other side of the Rio Grande where Norte-Americano law couldn't follow.

But they'd kept prime stock, stashed it away in a place on the edge of the badlands not far from where Boyard, the brains of the outfit, had finally built his ranch and had followed on from there, letting other pillagers — Dragoman and his boys for instance — do his stealing for him, no questions asked; and the place like a fortress. Had Boyard gotten too smart for his own good, too complacent? He couldn't give anybody the answer to that question now, and his old pard, Raithe (nobody ever called the redhead anything else) wouldn't ask any questions now, would stifle answers in blood and death.

"Do you think they'll be waiting for us?" a man asked.

"I don't know," the hard-bitten leader answered.

★ ★ ★

It hadn't been a very good hiding place after all, not when a seasoned hawk-eyed professional like Hardisty was the seeker for it. He got the boards up with his stout jack-knife, and there were the bulging saddle-bags. He dragged them out and opened them; and Annie's eyes started and she gave a little gasp.

Hardisty said, "Rip and his friend Black killed for that. Whether they planned to doublecross the rest of the gang I dunno — looks like the robbery and the cattle rustling was part of the same thing anyway. Hell, I'm sure o' that now. Black came to grief through sheer bad luck." Hardisty chuckled evilly. "I guess he sat on a rattler. But maybe if he hadn't Rip might have backshot him anyway. Lafe reckoned to find them here — maybe he was a double-crosser as well. Whether or not, him an' Rip fell out over the boodle and, honey, they just up an' killed each other."

Annie didn't say anything. She was still staring at the money. Hardisty wondered what was going through her mind. If he hadn't happened along and she had ultimately found the money herself what would she have done with it? He didn't ask her that question, which would've been pretty pointless after all, he figured. He said, "First thing I have to do is take this back where it came from. The rest will come later."

"I guess," said the girl softly.

He wasn't sure what she meant.

16

IT was night when they came. She was still at her cabin, though sleeping on a couch she had made up into a bed in the sitting-room, near the door and the window, as far as possible away from the bedroom where Lafe had been strangled to death after he had fired the shot that had ultimately caused Rip's death also.

Ceegar had wanted her to stay at his place but she had told him that nothing would drive her away from her home. She didn't know whether she was grieving for Rip: her emotions were all mixed up.

It had been good to see Max Hardisty again even under such tragic and mixed-up circumstances. How could she possibly compare Rip with such a man as Hardisty? Maybe if Hardisty had stayed . . .

But Marshal Hardisty and his two deputies had gone. He had said he would see her again. But would he?

When she heard the horses in the night, the hoofbeats waking her from an uneasy sleep, she thought it was Hardisty returning. Then, as she became fully awake, she chided herself for her fancies. Why would Hardisty return so soon?

She got from the couch and put on a thick wool robe which had been slung over a wooden chair. Her rifle was nearby also. She lifted it.

Somebody knocked at the door, which was very close to her. She padded in her bare feet, the rifle sloped in her right hand. Held that way it was heavy, but she was a strong girl. She opened the door with her left hand.

One man stood there, but there were others behind him, still mounted on their horses.

She was cagey and she was quick. With the door open fairly widely, she stood back from it and grasped the

Henry rifle in both hands and pointed it at the dark, scar-faced man in the doorway.

"There's no need to behave like that," he said. "I came looking for my three friends, Rip, Black and Lafe. I guess Lafe came here last. He was lookin' for the other two."

Although she'd only seen him once before, and that very briefly, she knew as he was speaking who he was.

"They're not here," she said.

"They came here." It was half-statement, half-question. He started to move forward.

She jerked the levelled rifle and said, "Stay right there. I'm quite prepared to use this."

"There's no need for that, girl. I told you . . . "

"I've seen Rip, and I've seen Lafe. Black hasn't been here. His body was left on the trail Rip told me. He'd been bitten by a rattler."

"If you're lying to me, girl . . . "

"Why would I lie?"

She didn't hear the man behind her till he spoke softly. "Put that down easily, honey, or I'll put a pill in your spine."

Her reactions were bewildered, but she knew she had to do what the man said. He must've come in through the outhouse! She bent and lowered the rifle to the floor with no sound at all.

The man in the doorway was grinning at her with wolfish teeth in the moonlight. Starke Dragoman, yes, that was who he was. The strange name seemed to suit him somehow. She should've shot him as soon as she saw him. But the men out there would have opened up then and she would be dead down there on her rifle.

Dragoman moved forward and she backed before him. The man moved aside from behind her and she didn't look at him, only catching a furtive glance at the gun he was holding, the steel glinting in the moonlight that came through the window.

She saw over Dragoman's shoulder

that the men outside were dismounting from their horses.

"Light a lamp," Dragoman said to the man with the gun. "Search the place." The man moved hastily. Dragoman picked up Annie's Henry rifle. "My, you're a feisty one, ain't you?" he said. He was grinning at her again, his teeth shining. Pure evil. The other men began to file through the door.

"Sit down," Dragoman said and he pointed to the couch, the improvised bed with the blanket tumbled on it.

She did as she was told, her legs feeling like water.

"If you're lying, girl . . . "

"I'm not lying."

"Did Rip and Lafe die, then?"

"They fought each other. They killed each other." I shouldn't have told him that, she thought, now he'll want to know why. But what else could she do? She went on, the words falling like stones. "Lafe's body is in an old barn out there." She pointed. "Rip's lying in a bedroom in Ceegar's place. I don't know where Black's body is."

Light blossomed. All the men were in the cabin now. One of them shut the door. "My, she's quite a piece, ain't she?" said another one.

Dragoman spoke his thoughts aloud then, asking the inevitable question. "If Rip an' Lafe fought, it must've been about the money. Where's the money, girl?"

"I don't know anything about any money." They were all around her now, pressing on her it seemed. Hardisty had the money. Could she tell them that? But she had already lied about that. To hell with them! But . . .

Dragoman bent over her, and he had a knife in his hand, brought from around his back as if by some trickery. With his free hand he pushed her back on the couch, that hand rising to her throat, gripping. She tried to kick him. "Hold her," he said.

Two of his men held her down while, with the knife, he stripped her flimsy garments from her after slashing the belt of her robe. The men clustered around. Their hands seemed to be everywhere. Their eyes gleamed in the moonlight.

"Back off," snarled Dragoman and, reluctantly, they did so.

Dragoman took his left hand away from her throat and she gulped air. She flinched as, with his other hand, he pressed the cold blade of the knife in the place where his left hand had been a split moment before. He said, "If you don't tell me what I want to know, I'm gonna let the boys have you, one by one . . . "

There were murmurs, chuckles, grunts of satisfaction. The men moved again. "Cut it," snarled their leader and they shuffled, then became still, silent, waiting.

"And that isn't all," went on Dragoman. "After the boys have had their fill I'm gonna start cuttin' on you. When I've finished I don't reckon any of 'em would want you any more. Or any other man want you for that matter — you'll be useless, girl."

He turned the blade of the knife around and pricked her throat. She felt the warm blood running down her body and between her breasts.

"You boys back off," Dragoman said. "I'll tell you who's gonna be first, an' the next, an' the next." He turned and looked at the man who had menaced Annie from behind, who had lit the hurricane lantern, the light now bathing the room in a yellow effulgence.

"I think Dobey should have first turn."

Dobey was young and burly and had a squint eye and broken teeth when he grinned, his fingers fumbling as he started to unbuckle his belt.

The knife was away from Annie's throat. She kicked Dragoman in the crotch. Her feet were bare, but her aim was good. He dropped the knife and staggered backwards, clutching at himself. The knife was on the bottom of the couch. Annie grabbed it.

Dobey was caught in a frozen attitude, the top of his pants open but his hands still gripping them as if he had suddenly become very shy. His mouth was open.

One of the other men made a grab for Annie and she slashed outwards with the naked blade, almost taking the end of the feller's nose off. The man backed violently, cannoning into one of his pards.

Another man had his gun out — a reflex action — but didn't seem to know what to do with it. Momentarily, everybody seemed rooted. Dragoman was straightening up, but he was still gasping for breath.

"Goddammit," he panted. "Hold the bitch."

Annie moved the gleaming blade in an arc in front of her. Then one of the men said, "There's somebody comin'."

From the window, peering out, another man said, "It's riders an' they're comin' in the same way as

161

we did." He pressed his face closer to the window and uttered a string of obscenities.

"Damn your hide," said Dragoman. "Can you see who it is?"

"A bunch from the ranch. An' in front of 'em is that ol' redheaded son-a-bitch . . . "

"Raithe," said Dragoman.

"Yeh, an' I thought he was dead. I thought he was stomped by the herd."

"Well, he ain't no ghost," said Dragoman. "They're all human, an' we can take 'em."

17

WHEN ordered by his chief, Dobey doused the lamp which he'd lit a bit earlier. Then he fastened his pants and buckled up his belt.

The cabin was in darkness except for the moonlight coming through the window.

The horses and riders outside were very much in the worst position. Seeing the lighted cabin, Raithe's fury had led him on too precipitately; and his men had followed him.

The moonlight was so bright that the folks inside the cabin could see the horsemen's faces.

With the cabin light going out, the horses were milling as the men, obviously at an order from their leader, split apart, making lesser targets. But targets they still were.

There was no cover out there. Behind the horses and men the narrow creek was like a silver ribbon in the moonlight.

There had been a sort of jumbled lull — then the horses were moving again, gathering speed, their riders now low in their saddles.

"They're tryin' to cut in round us," Dragoman yelled.

He smashed the cabin window with the barrel of his gun, which he then levelled, steadying it with the fingers of his other hand at the wrist.

Annie made a run for the outhouse door but Dobey grabbed her.

Half-turning his head, Dragoman was startled, hesitant. He fired off two rapid shots but his aim had been slightly deflected and he didn't think he'd hit anything. He swore obscenely.

"Hold 'er!" he yelled.

Annie was fighting Dobey, but his strength was too much for her and she was naked: he was bruising her, his hands brutal, seeking her vulnerable parts. She was flung back on the couch and Dobey's fingers were busy with his buttons again, an anticipatory gleam in his eyes in the moonlight.

"Cut it," said Dragoman who wasn't missing anything now but wanted to keep shooting. "Keep your hands off her. Keep your gun on her and slug her if she won't keep still."

Frustration made Dobey awkward, fumbling. But finally he had his gun out and he pointed it at the girl mirrored in the moonlight from the window spearing past the men, the defenders. The attackers were firing now. Bullets came through the window as Dragoman moved quickly to one side.

The girl was out of the line of fire, half-crouching, a picture of soft curves and blazing defiant eyes. Dobey got down on one knee as he covered her with levelled .45.

Men were at the door of the cabin, had it part-open, were trying to fire at the wheeling horsemen who were attacking like Indians.

Dobey fell sideways, awkward on one knee, as a bullet scored his right shoulder — and he was a right-handed man. His shirt-sleeve was torn. The bullet burned his flesh. He dropped the gun and Annie rolled off her couch and reached for it. But Dragoman, who suddenly seemed to have eyes in the back of his head, was quicker, turning like a striking rattlesnake.

He hit the girl on her temple with the barrel of his heavy gun and she sprawled face downwards, an erotic picture, but then very still. Dobey picked up his gun and remained on both knees looking down stupidly at the girl.

"She'll be no trouble for a while," snarled Dragoman. "Lift her back on the couch. Then come an' help out, goddammit."

Dobey obeyed orders. Then, holding his gun gingerly, he joined Dragoman at the window, both of them peering around corners, trying to draw some sort of a bead on fast-moving horsemen, moving like wraiths in the moonlight, a bewildering quality now.

A man staggered backwards from the partially open door, his face half-obliterated by a heavy slug, the blood like a glistening black mass in the moonlight before the shadows engulfed him and he lay flat on the boards and deathly still.

At Dragoman's orders, men were keeping a watch at back of the building. But the attackers were not digging in: they were fighting like Apaches, moving, *moving. Moving.* Sending blistering fire on the cabin. Trying to penetrate the door, the square of the window with shattered glass gleaming in the moonlight.

Dragoman's forehead had been cut by flying glass and he had to keep wiping the blood which ran into his eyes and in spidery trails down his scarred, lantern-jawed face.

He dragged his bandanna from around his throat and used it in his left hand to staunch the blood, stop it. He levelled his gun in his right hand and tried to draw a bead on a horseman he recognized as the hard-bitten, redheaded foreman called Raithe. And Raithe paused, waving a gun in his right hand in some kind of signal. He seemed to be shouting and there was a lull in the firing, but the words couldn't be heard in the inside of the cabin which was full of gunsmoke.

Raithe was momentarily limned in the moonlight. Like the statue of a mounted Civil War general in a town square. An intrepid soldier calling his troops on. But this statue was no statue, was living flesh and blood, and, for one split moment, incredibly vulnerable, a prime target. And Dragoman, at his window, squeezed the trigger of his Colt and sent a lethal slug spinning through the still air, the gun bucking satisfactorily in his fist but he knowing that, this time, his aim was straight and true.

★ ★ ★

The searing bullet bored through the side of Raithe's head and upwards a little, destroying his brain and exiting on the other side almost at his crown and taking his battered Stetson with it, wheeling under the bright moon and, snatched by a small breeze, taken almost to the waters of the creek but then nestling like a bird on the banks. Raithe should have been propelled from his horse: he was pushed to one side though, and then he swayed backwards like a puppet with broken strings in a fit-up show: his feet were caught in his stirrups. His body bent sideways then, however, and his horse bolted, Raithe's body still swaying backwards and forwards grotesquely, loosely, horribly. And then the horse hit the creek and the body came loose completely and flopped in the water, though it didn't sink as the creek was very shallow at this time.

The riderless horse galloped wildly

onwards and was taken by fugitive shadows barred by spears of yellow moonlight. There was something eerie about the whole scene. And it was as if the attackers had been momentarily transfixed by the sight, that it had filled them with superstition and terror.

They broke out suddenly as if they would gather up the body of their dead leader from the waters.

Two of them did actually do this while the rest flung shots back at the dark cabin.

Men inside the cabin opened up with rifles. A rider was propelled from his horse and fell in the shadows but scrambled to his feet, water streaming from him, ran limping after his horse, caught him, remounted.

"They're running out," shouted a man by the door of the cabin.

Another man was coughing violently. A third man started to laugh but he, too, was taken up by a spasm of coughing as the gunsmoke entered his open mouth. A fourth man flung the door wide and the fresh air streamed in.

The erstwhile attackers were streaming away, their horses galloping wildly, on the other side of the creek. They had taken Raithe's body with them. But another body, very still and like a bundle of old clothes, lay on the settlement side of the creek not far from the Stetson that had escaped from the dead foreman's head.

A man ran through from the back of the cabin, yelling, "The townies are comin'." Dragoman turned to other men, said, "Hold 'em off."

Annie had come to her senses, was looking dazedly about her in the moonlight. Dragoman bent over her, his gun pouched, his knife in his hand again.

"One last chance, girl," he said thickly. "Where's the money? Answer me quickly or I'll kill you out of hand anyway."

She was beaten, trying to save her own life, but knowing she might lose it anyway. She took a chance for salvation. "Max Hardisty has the money," she whispered.

"Marshal Hardisty of Commoddee?"

"Yes."

A man yelled. "Them goddam townies are loaded for bear."

"We can't waste time fighting them as well," said Dragoman. "Let's get out of here."

"How about the girl?" said Dobey.

"Leave 'er."

18

CEEGAR comforted her. He wrapped her tightly in the blanket and held her while she sobbed and shook. He had never seen tough, pretty Annie in a state like this before.

But he knew the cause as she talked to him brokenly; and he understood.

"I let him down, old friend," she said. "Him and his two friends. I sent that scum after them."

"You knew he had a good start, honey," Ceegar told her. "That bunch can't possibly catch up."

"But they're makin' for Commoddee. They . . ."

But he cut in on her. "I know Commoddee and its people. And I know Hardisty. I knew him before you did. He's more than a match for Starke Dragoman any time."

"I shouldn't have told them. I . . . "

"You're talkin' nonsense, my girl," said Ceegar with sternness now. "You had to tell them. I reckon Dragoman would've gotten it figured anyway sooner or later. They would've done what he said, treated you very badly. And then they would've killed you. Scum like that don't play by any rules. You're lucky you're alive now. Dragoman would've killed you out of hand if the fancy took him."

"If you hadn't come along . . . "

"We heard the shooting o' course. That bunch didn't waste any more time — they lit out like Ol Nick was on their tails."

She laughed then, and it was kind of a strange sound. But she was no longer shaking, and she'd quit sobbing.

"That's my girl," said Ceegar and he took out one of his long weeds from his vest pocket.

"I'll light it for you," she said, sitting up with her blanket wrapped around her.

He gave her his box of lucifers and she struck one and put the flame to the end of the cigar and he puffed. How many times had she done this for him? He was like the father she'd never known, or a tough, kindly, understanding uncle.

"I'll tell you what I'll do, honey," he said, his head half-turned as he puffed blue smoke away from her. "I'll take two of my boys and we'll go to the railhead. We can leave our horses there and hop a train. There's a coach that picks up at the other end an' goes to Commoddee. Or we can hire more horses there. Hell, Max is my friend too, ain't he? I ought to do somep'n. And I'd sure like to bring Dragoman and his trash down."

"I'll come with you," Annie said.

"No, I won't have that." Ceegar's voice was stern again. "Max wouldn't want it either. Hell, you sort of stood in between him an' that bunch, didn't you, givin' him a good start? You hadn't thought of it that way, had you?"

"I guess not."

"I could be in Commoddee even before Max an' his two deputies. I could certainly be there before the Dragoman bunch. I'll take my two best boys. You ought to go to my place an' stay there till we get back, huh?"

"All right," said the girl, more like her old self now. "I'll run the roulette wheel. It won't be the first time I've done that, will it?"

"Nope."

There was a knock on the door. Ceegar got up from the edge of the couch and opened the door. "It's Emma," he said over his shoulder and he backed off.

A fat elderly lady bustled in, said, "I got here as soon as I could. I was back behind the other end of town with Cissie Pounter and her kids — two of 'em are ailing again . . . Oh, you poor dear." She almost flung herself at Annie. But as Annie and Ceegar well knew, the tireless Emma was mighty good with folk and what ailed 'em, and she had a heart as big as a bucket.

Ceegar said, "I'll leave you ladies an' go back to the place. You get dressed, Annie, an' then come back with Emma. I'll be leavin', so don't take too long."

"We won't," said Annie.

"Go on with you," said Emma.

Wished we had got here earlier, thought Ceegar, and we could have gotten after those bastards. But they had too big a start. All the boys were back at their doings now, but he knew where to find the two he needed. He hastened his steps.

★ ★ ★

She was redheaded Nita; and she was quite a big noise in Commoddee now. An establishment lady no less, and prospering. She didn't think it was exactly the life she had planned for herself. What had she planned? Hell, she had never planned.

Folks called her Miss Nita. But she

knew that there were others who didn't know her so well and referred to her as 'Hardisty's woman'. She didn't like that much.

She had known many other men before she met Hardisty. When they met he'd been a paid gunfighter (Hell, he still was!) and she was an outlaw girl running with a bunch dubbed sardonically Luke and his Lads. Luke had been an ugly, murderous cuss. But Nita had been his woman.

Hardisty had been running with that strange Indian girl he had saved from scalping by a bunch of white settlers. Charley Scar and his Apaches had been on the warpath at that time and, as far as the settlers were concerned, any Injun was better as a dead 'un. But Luke and his renegades hadn't been any better than any Injun . . . [1]

God, that seemed a long time ago.

_____
[1] See *The Plains Rats*

Like another life. The owlhoot life. *The restlessness* . . .

And, lately, Nita had been fighting that restlessness like it was invisible whips driving her. And Hardisty was out on the trail again. He would kill or be killed. He was *killing* his restlessness.

She waited for him to return, and she worried about him and wanted him.

But did she want him? She had done things, many things, without him. A sort of perversity made her want to pack her bags and run. And then another side of her made her wait.

She was surprised when Ceegar and his two partners turned up at her place. They had been to the marshal's office and had been told that Hardisty hadn't been there for some time, was away, hadn't got back. They'd been half-expecting that. But had Nita seen him yet? Yes, she thought sardonically, I'm Hardisty's woman, maybe he would come here first.

But he hadn't, and she told them so.

Then they told her why they were here and she had to do some fast thinking.

She made Ceegar and his friends welcome and they all waited. The whole town seemed to be waiting.

Ceegar and his two boys left Nita's place after a wash-up and a quick meal. They seemed fidgety, as well they might be. They remounted the horses they had hired at the rail-station a few miles away and they ranged the town and its outskirts. And Nita waited in trepidation.

Hardisty and his pards were, it seemed, later than might have been expected.

★ ★ ★

The burying of Rip and Lafe could hardly be called a funeral. They had a plot side by side because Annie thought that was fitting. Folks liked Annie and had to admit that that girl had been through a lot lately. Folks would have been inclined to say dig a hole an' throw 'em both in it and cover it up; it didn't seem fittin' in fact that they should be buried in Boot Hill and have a grave apiece.

The settlement's graveyard was just a barren hillside and there were some nefarious sort buried there among the better people who had only sought peace in this comparatively isolated place in the wide, wild lands. But they had all been part of this place and Rip and Lafe never had.

But folks did what Annie wanted, knowing that Ceegar, who was Annie's friend would want what she wanted. And, right now, Ceegar was the grand high panjandrum around here.

Ceegar was not of course present at the funeral, if it could be called that. There was no church, no preacher. There were a couple of semi-inebriated gravediggers, and Annie and two of Ceegar's boys who were watching over Annie, and a few hangers-on who had nothing else to do right then.

It seemed to them that Annie was a mite crestfallen now, even a mite ashamed, her head bent, her long dark hair hiding her pretty face. It seemed she said a few words, but they weren't audible, and the clods began to fall.

Those folks were going back to their chores, or whatever, when the dusty drifter on the dusty horse drifted in.

★ ★ ★

Although the folks in the settlement hadn't known it, there'd been a funeral also in Commoddee. A more salubrious place. And this had been a *proper* funeral with plenty of mourners, a carriage with four black horses, a little feller in front beating a drum slowly and the mourners walking slowly behind in the time-honoured way.

The chief mourner at the funeral of young Tod Millen had been rancher Bill Dakell, for Tod had been his foreman and his friend. The two men who had murdered Tod had taken

Bill's money also as well as the life of the boy who had been like a son to him. But the money was of no consequence.

With Bill was Rancher Smithon, from whom Bill had had the money for the cattle that had been driven to the Commoddee territory and, in a fell swoop, that had been stolen also. The two ranchers hadn't known each other particularly well, had just been protagonists in a decent deal. But in this last go-down they had stood side by side like old friends, neither of them knowing whether the money would be gotten back, or the cattle, though it hardly seemed likely in either case.

They had both been members of a posse which had finally returned to town empty-handed. And there'd been some burying to do. Smithon's foreman, Jed Spokes had gone out on the murder and robbery trail, with him one of Dakell's hands, Aldo Boner; and they were under the guidance of Commoddee's fighting marshal Max

Hardisty, and if he couldn't drag something out of this mess nobody could.

The rest had been told to wait. They waited and wondered . . .

Some of them saw Ceegar from Ceegar's Place out on the prairie. Not all of them knew him though, or the two hard-bitten younkers who accompanied him.

Nobody told them anything . . .

19

ON account of the battle at the settlement one of Dragoman's boys had a hole in his side. It had been patched up on the trail but this had had to be done fast and after a while the wound began to bleed again and the man was weak and whining, slumping in the saddle like something half-dead.

"Quit your belly-achin'," Dragoman snarled. "That ain't nothin' but a bug-bite."

"It's runnin' away from me," the man moaned. "It's just purely runnin' away from me."

His one boot was full of blood and his sodden shirt-tails stuck to him. He'd meant the blood, yes, the blood. It was draining from him and taking his life with it. He was partly delirious: his moaning and whining became an unintelligible mumble.

When he fell from his horse, the others reined in and one of them dismounted and got down beside him. The wounded man seemed to be pleading for mercy.

The other man didn't say anything to him, but looked back and upwards. Then he said, "He's pretty far gone, chief."

"We'll have to leave him then. We can't tote him. We can't stop an' do anything else for him." Dragoman chuckled evilly. "'Cept shoot him. And that," he added, "wouldn't be a clever thing to do, the way a gunshot 'ud carry in these open spaces."

But the boys didn't need him to tell them that. They shuffled impatiently, and the horses shuffled too. "Cut 'is throat," said Dragoman.

"I ain't gonna cut 'is throat," said the dismounted man. The man beneath him was a sort of pard of his.

"Godammit, leave 'im then," said the unpredictable leader. "Get back on your horse an' let's get movin'."

The man hesitated but then climbed back into the saddle. The others started off and he followed them.

He didn't know — none of them did — that a certain drifter who'd called in briefly at the settlement and then left it again, was already on the trail behind them.

The Dragoman rider didn't know — none of them did — that when the drifter reached the dying man, the latter was still alive.

A dying man, still with all his gear even — as if he and all that he carried had been tossed carelessly aside. But no horse of course. A horse was too precious to be left to roam.

For a human, this was a sorry way to end. He had gone across the badlands with the stolen cattle. With Dragoman and the rest he had come back through the badlands, then having to take a longer route, a roundabout one because the pass through the hills had been deliberately blocked after they came through the first time. But because they didn't have a herd any more it had been an easier journey as badlands journeys go.

But then at the settlement the man had stopped a bullet and that had been the start of it. And the end of it!

He lay and cursed Dragoman who had left him to die: he had just enough life left in him to do that. There were no more journeys left for him but the final one.

Oh, yes, with his pards — not one of them could've tried to save him, thus incurring Dragoman's wrath, vengeance even — he had travelled fast. And, if it hadn't been for the battle in the settlement . . .

But the drifter had travelled faster.

It could be said he was no drifter after all.

He had come through the badlands like a bat out of hell. He hadn't slowed his pace at all except for the short break in the settlement. He had lingered briefly, had been spotted briefly, had gone on as if the Devil drove him.

The dying man and he had both come a long way over dangerous dusty trails.

One lived for revenge, for the taking of life.

Now the other seemed to welcome death, having a freedom from pain now, having the strange lucidity that sometimes comes before death.

He looked into the drifter's eyes and told him all he wanted to know. Then he died and the drifter left him and rode on as fast as ever.

★ ★ ★

Annie was handling the roulette wheel in the Gambling Hell at Ceegar's Place and, except for the absence of Ceegar and two of his boys things were going on again pretty much as they'd done before.

Folks drifted in. Out again. If they hadn't been told tales by garrulous oldsters they wouldn't have known that anything untoward had happened here in recent times.

A man came here to hide, to rest, and, whether lawless or otherwise, drifting or on the run, often to turn the cards, spin the wheel, 'buck the tiger' . . .

★ ★ ★

They were a tired bunch of outlaws now. Even their slave-driving leader had to admit this.

The horses were lagging. They had been going hell-for-leather hard and long over rough trails and they couldn't go much further without rest. They were heavy-eyed and blowing.

Dragoman knew where he was going. Maybe it would be best not to go in fast. Hell, fast was the last thing they'd be able to do if they didn't bide their time. Dragoman called a halt and men almost fell out of their saddle and even welcomed the hard ground on their aching limbs.

"We'll stay here till nightfall," Dragoman told them.

By nightfall most of them were asleep, so, unusually for him he leaned to them. He gave them more time — after putting two men on watch, to be changed at approximately hourly intervals until he decided they should all move again.

The night was sultry and dark with the moon only peeping fitfully through clouds now and then like a slice of well-sucked lemon. The stars were so high they gave little light at all and there was silence except for the snoring and shifting of aching, restless men who had suffered tension and peril too long.

They had camped in a slight dip where here and there they could find softer ground and lay their saddle blankets. There were a few trees half-ringing the tops of the slopes and the two watchers, who were still tired, sat against a trunk apiece with their rifles at their sides.

The land around them was undulating, broken by outcrops of rocks and shrubberies and patches of long grass interspersed with uneven rocky ground. There were places of shapes and shadows.

The slow-moving clouds and the intermittent moonlight played tricks with men's eyes, causing the drowziness of the two men — and the bloodthirsty threats of their leader were forgotten — to be slowly intensified. They tried to keep vigilant until their hour was up — and one of them had a precious and much-vaunted gold half-hunter which he'd found during an express office robbery: he kept glancing at this till it slipped from his lax fingers and his eyelids slid like blinds over his somnolent eyes.

He hardly felt the sharp blade of the knife as it slid over his throat and slashed it deeply from ear to ear. Before he could make any kind of a sound, he was dead, and his killer crouched beside him, hidden from the other watcher by the trunk of the tree.

The other watcher made a snuffling sound certainly not a sound that might have been made by an individual who was wide awake. The man with the bloodstained knife waited a while longer before beginning to move again, using all the cover he could find, crawling sinuously like a snake in the grass.

He reached the other man at his tree, and some half-awakening sixth sense sent a warning to the dozing man's brain and he stirred, turned towards the crawling menace that had crept up behind him.

His right hand reached for his hand-gun but, even as his fingers closed over the butt, the knife drove into his breast while a hand was clasped over his mouth and nose, tightening like a vice.

One hand held his face, stifling any cry he tried to make. The knife was driven in to the hilt as the dying man was forced back hard against the tree until his killer let go, letting the body slide down into the grass, the head twisting round the trunk of the tree, the staring eyes becoming hidden.

The killer wiped his knife on the pants leg that was stretched out in front of him and returned the shining weapon to his belt. He turned away and began to crawl.

20

IT was a day and night of hard-riding men and hard-driven horses. Hardisty and his two deputies had expected to be in Commoddee by early nightfall. But that was not to be. The malicious fates saw things differently than that.

It was dusk and the clouds were low as if presaging rain when Jed Spokes' horse stumbled and had a nasty fall, throwing his rider.

Jed, like most cowhands — and he was a foreman — was a good rider. But he'd been drowzing in the saddle over fairly even ground and was taken completely by surprise. He hit the ground hard and the horse, legs flailing, almost rolled over him.

The man was stunned but managed to climb to his feet. But then he began to wander about in circles, cursing without making much sense, the words a mumble.

It turned out that the horse was better off than the man, was certainly lucky that he hadn't broken a leg and had had to be put down. Shooting a gun off was something that the boys wouldn't want to do — and any Western man would be grieved to lose a good horse.

Hardisty got down from his saddle and caught hold of Jed and brought him to a standstill. Jed was brought to more awareness and said, "Goddammit, I can walk by myself."

"Do it then," snapped the marshal, never noted for his patience.

He got back on his own horse and let Jed hold on to his stirrup. The tall man rode slowly for a while, with young Aldo Boner uttering jocular comments from the sidelines.

Jed began to take umbrage and Hardisty said, "Leave him be," and Aldo shut up.

The riderless horse had a cut on

his neck where he'd hit the rock, a loose piece over which he'd actually stumbled in the first place as it became dislodged from the earth and rolled under his hooves. Hardisty had patched the wound with moss and it had adhered to the flesh. The horse now was even stepping lively, unshaken, his trembles gone, behaving as if nothing had happened to him.

Jed looked back at him and said, "Look at 'im. He doesn't know how damn' lucky he's been. I'm gonna ride him now." He let go of Hardisty's stirrup and the tall man said, "I thought his gait had gone a bit loppy. Take care with him."

"I know what I'm doin'," retorted Jed petulantly as he mounted the horse.

He was just being bloody-minded as he was bound to be, nursing his bruises, but his head clear now. He was a good horseman who loved horses. He rode slowly, carefully, with Hardisty and Boner a little ahead of him but matching their pace to his.

It was an almost sedate cortège and the two men in front could hear the man behind them talking softly to his mount. Like many of his kind he obviously preferred a four-footed pard to most humans — and actually they couldn't bring themselves to blame him for that, not after the horrendous things that had happened lately due to humankind.

* * *

The drifter lay on his belly and looked down into the grassy hollow and the men and horses gathered there, no campfire, and men spread about in indolent attitudes while their mounts grazed.

They had guards, this lot, they thought everything was ace-high; they'd move again when their leader said the word. The light wasn't good and the man at the top of the slope couldn't spot the leader, figured he must be lying down someplace, maybe sheltered by one or the other of his men. The drifter didn't let this faze him, though. He thought fast; and now he began to move his arms, fast, without raising from his belly-flattened position.

The grass around him at this spot was long, made for good concealment. He began to tear at the long stalks of grass. He got himself a bundle pretty quickly and rolled it into a ball. He put his rifle within prime reach and then he struck a lucifer and lit the frayed edges of the ball of dry, brittle grass.

It was rolling down the slope, a ball of fire, before anybody spotted it; then a yell went up. But by then the drifter had his rifle at his shoulder.

The first man was on his feet. The drifter drew a bead on the gesticulating figure and pressed the trigger.

The standing man was hit in the side of the head and spun around forcibly before falling like a weak and splintered tree.

Another outlaw, up on his knees, was hit in the face, was slammed backwards and then, as his knees held him, jerked forward again and finished up in a grotesque curled position.

More grass had caught fire and was blazing merrily, illuminating the dip as if it were an Halloween party that was taking place down there. A very noisy party now.

The drifter didn't really have much cover, and, if he stood up, would be limned against the growing flames. He knew he had hit two men — both of whom could be dead — and dropped another one who was crawling, screaming. He wriggled backwards, firing indiscriminately, emptying his rifle then dragging it with one hand while he drew his hand-gun with the other. The outlaws were firing back at him and the bullets were coming perilously close. He swung himself round, wriggling. A slug took the heel off his riding boot. Another scored a line along his leg. He felt the burn of it, then the blood began to seep through his pants.

Men began to climb the slopes. They weren't using rifles, had their hand-guns ready. They seemed to know now that they were only menaced by one lone marksman — and the rifle-fire seemed to have finished anyway. They flung blistering fire up at the ridge above them.

The drifter couldn't move very fast: not as fast as any snake in the grass, moving on his belly as he was, no way for a man to fight, unnatural.

He raised himself upwards a bit and began to crawl and that was when he was hit in the side with a shot from the levelled Colt of a man who'd come diagonally up the slope and fired a lucky one which paid off. The drifter's body jerked as a gasp of pain was ejected from his open, panting mouth. With a desperate lurch he jerked himself to his feet and ran, bent over, weaving from side to side, his hand-gun holstered, his rifle swinging in his right hand, his left pressed to the burning, bloody wound in his side.

Bullets winged around, but he was away from the light of the burning grass now and visibility wasn't good. Slugs zipped by him like angry bees but he wasn't hit again. He reached his horse who'd been waiting in a spare cluster of trees and he clambered in the saddle.

"C'mon, boy," he whispered. "C'mon now."

The cayuse responded, a smudgy paint who could go like the wind when he felt like it; and his master's desperate urgency was communicated to him now. The man didn't guide him, let him run, only trying to get away from the pursuit that he figured would be gotten under way now. He had to put as much distance away from that as he could, find someplace to hide and check his wound, not knowing how bad it was. But now he fought waves of nausea and the lowering clouds seemed to be pressing down on him. Then he felt the rain begin to fall, thin, cool. He was glad of it. He let the horse carry him — and the gallant little cayuse who'd come far and hard, seemed to have taken on a new life. Pass it on to me, boy, the drifter thought, pass it on to me . . .

★ ★ ★

"I thought I heard gunfire," Aldo Boner said.

"Might've been thunder," said Max Hardisty as the first drops of rain began to fall.

"This ain't thunderstorm rain," Boner said.

From behind the two, Jed Spokes said, "Yeh, I thought I heard somep'n that sounded like gunfire. But it could've been thunder I guess."

Marshal Hardisty reined in. Boner, a little in front, looked back, followed the lawman's example, brought his horse back to the other two as Spokes caught up and they sat in the saddles and listened. The rain came faster but still thinly, refreshing horses and men, hissing, making a comforting sound.

There was no wind. There was no thunder either, and no gunshots in the distance, in the sprawling vastness that would carry sound.

They donned their slickers to protect them if the rain became faster, though it showed no signs of doing so. They carried on slowly, heads down. Then young Aldo, who seemed to have better hearing than either of the older men, reined in again.

"Not more shooting or thunder?" said Hardisty sardonically.

"Sounded like hoofbeats," said Aldo.

Then all three men were still again, seated on still horses.

"I hear it," said Jed Spokes.

"Me too," said Hardisty.

"I told you!" cried Aldo Boner.

21

HARDISTY dismounted from his horse and got down on one knee and leaned and bent his head sideways.

"Only one horse I think," he said. "Although there is a sort of rumble so there may be others further back, or even a few cattle."

Jed Spokes dismounted stiffly, carefully, still feeling his aches and bruises after his fall, which might have incapacitated a weaker man. He even managed to get even lower than the marshal and at length he said, "Don't sound much like cattle to me, though there could be more horses."

"We'll wait," said Hardisty and they both remounted. Aldo Boner already had his Colt in his hand, and now the other two followed his example.

The lone horse and its rider came

out of the thin-veiled rainy night with dramatic suddenness. The small paint horse was going as if driven by the wind, though there was very little of that with the rain. Now Aldo was the quicker of the three men, sliding from his horse and rushing forward, grabbing the reins of the beast, drawing it to an abrupt halt so that the man on its back was almost pitched from the saddle.

The little paint was snorting. The horseman was clinging to the beast's neck.

"He's hurt," said Hardisty, dismounting.

Jed Spokes stayed in the saddle. He'd had his fill tonight of leaving the saddle, forcibly at one time, and getting back on again, felt he mightn't make it this time.

Between them Hardisty and Boner eased the wounded man down. "His side," said Hardisty. "Careful." Both of them were becoming smeared with the wounded rider's blood. The horse was tired, stood now docilely with head hanging.

Hardisty, who had already proved that he was the medicine-man of the three, got down beside the man on the ground and looked up at Boner and said, "Go back a bit. Listen."

The younger man nodded, went awkwardly on high-heeled riding boots, bent, dropped on one knee. From the saddle Jed Spokes said, "I can't hear anything now."

Aldo stayed where he was for a little longer then straightened himself, came back. "I can't hear anything either. If there was somep'n else, horses, cattle, whatever, it's stopped. Mebbe it's been swallowed by the ground."

"It's wet, it's gettin' softer," said Spokes. "If there's anything comin' now we'd've heard it."

Hardisty was on his feet, by his horse, rummaging in his saddle-bags. He came up with some cloth. He returned to Boner and the man on the ground, said, "I'll do the best I can. An' then we'll have to get him to Commoddee as fast as we can. Looks like he's been shot in the side. But how or when is a goddam mystery."

"Do you know him?" asked Boner.

"Funny you should say that. He looks kinda familiar, but I can't rightly place the jib. If I've seen it before maybe it was quite a while ago."

"An owlhooter maybe?"

"Who knows?"

★ ★ ★

Starke Dragoman wondered, who was that maniac?

A shooting wild man. A good shot too, and there were two dead men to prove it, and one wounded.

"I got 'im," said one of the other men. "I'm sure I got 'im."

"Maybe he'll fall outa the saddle an' die then," said the leader sardonically, nastily. "Whether or not, I ain't gonna chase him any more."

Dragoman's cunning mind was

working again. He was unhurt, had been fast asleep when the shooting started. He had lain low. He had taken a shot at the elusive marksman and had known he'd missed.

Still and all, though he as leader wouldn't have admitted it to the cuss who'd just bragged about his own shooting, he was pretty sure that the marksman had been hit and was no longer any danger to them.

"The horses have been ridden too hard," he said. "Their rest and ours was disturbed by that crazy man and his long gun. We've gotta take stock an' we've gotta rest if we gonna carry on an' do what I planned to do."

That was kind of a long speech for him, laying it out for the boys, something he didn't usually do. But he hadn't actually laid it all out, had he? The alarm would be given in Commoddee, and he hadn't got enough men now to go in hell-for-leather, even if he'd had that planned at first — and he had to admit to himself now he hadn't actually been sure about that. Now he had to be more devious and that suited him mightily, he told himself. There was money in that town, and loot. And Max Hardisty, who would have to be put down . . .

* * *

Max was back: Nita knew it. She had been worried. She had heard horses in the night and she had gotten out of her bed and gone to the window and looked out on Main Street. The rain that had been falling, hissing against her window during her restless slumbering, had quietened down and, though there was still darkness, the darker clouds had scudded away and visibility was better.

Nita saw the four horsemen and she recognized Hardisty, and the foreman called Jed and the younger man whom she didn't know so well but had heard called Aldo. The fourth man was, she thought, a stranger to her and he didn't seem to be riding right, was awkward in the saddle almost as if he'd been tied there. Was he sick? Or was he a prisoner?

Nita wanted to put on her clothes and go down and get an answer to those questions. But she forced herself not to do this, knowing that Max wouldn't like it, wouldn't want her to get involved. And it seemed that Max himself was all right. He had been erect in the saddle a little ahead of the others. He had ridden like he always rode, and now all four of the men and horses were out of sight down the street, making for the jail, or maybe the doctor's place.

Nita went and lay in her bed again. But she didn't sleep. She had too much on her mind — and dark forebodings which she couldn't dispel. And a terrible feeling of guilt . . .

★ ★ ★

211

"I can fix it," the doc said.

And the man on the cot began to mumble.

The other three men leaned closer.

The wounded man shut up, his eyes squinched tight. He was still as a post again and they couldn't hear him breathing.

The doc bent and put his ear to the patient's chest.

Hardisty began, "Is it . . . ?"

"Quiet," snapped the Doc.

There was dead silence. Even the marshal took heed of the cantankerous but highly capable old sawbones.

The doc straightened up, pushing his spectacles back on to the bridge of his nose. "He's out. He's resting the way he should. Give me a chance to do what I want to do for him. Get out of here, all of you, and let me do what I have to do."

Hardisty said, "Don't you need any help, Doc?"

"Not right now, thank you."

"All right, boys, let's go." Hardisty

led the two other men from the room. He was frustrated, badly needed for the wounded boy to come to his senses and talk.

But there were other things the marshal had to do also, other folks he had to see. He'd been told who was here — and he'd met briefly with Ceegar and his two boys who were waiting on the edge of town, wouldn't budge: Hardisty's old fighting friend was adamant about that.

Rancher Bill Dakell was back in town, stopping over after attending the funeral of his murdered foreman Tod Millen. The local rancher Smithon, Jed Spokes's boss, was also in town. Bill Dakell's sidekick, Texas Joe Elliwell was here with his boss, who was also Aldo Boner's boss of course. They would all be handy if needed — and things could well turn out that way. Boner and Spokes were both eager to stay with the marshal and continue to act as his deputies, and he didn't argue with them about that: they had proved their worth.

He ranged the town. He placed his men. There were plenty of volunteers. They had rested. Now it was his and his deputies' turn to rest. They dossed down like cats in the law office while the night drew towards the dawn.

22

"**I**TS dawn," one of the men said. "Ain't it too light to go in there now, chief?"

"No, it'll be too late if we leave it, I'm thinking now," Dragoman said. "They'd expect somep'n by night if they expect anything at all."

"If that snapshootin' bastard got through to here he could've warned 'em," said another member of the band.

"Why would he? Who was he? Maybe he's dead. And, if he ain't, maybe he'll be avoiding places like Commoddee anyway. It used to be so peaceable — with Marshal Max Hardisty an' all!" Dragoman gave a spurt of harsh laughter. He was doing a bit of explaining, which was unusual for him. But it was evident to his depleted followers that he'd made up his mind about something. And that something might be that they go right in. But how?

He told them. Asking a question first off. "None o' you boys are known in Commoddee, are you?"

None of them were. One said he'd been in the town once, drifted through. He didn't know anybody there and nobody knew him.

"Drift in now then," said Dragoman. "Just like waddies lookin' for work. Straight on now." He pointed. They could see the outer edges of the town. He went on, "I'm gonna leave you. I'm making a detour and going in through the back. I know a way. And I know somebody I can visit there as well. If you hear shootin' it'll be in the middle of town, off Main Street. And you come a-riding, y'understand? Believe me, there are great pickin's here."

He carried them. They had to follow his way, the way of pillage and murder. He grinned at them wolfishly and they were ready. Then he was gone.

He was wary that folks might be on lookout at the back. But this was a drowzy dawning and many folks would still be asleep, he counted on that. He knew a stand of cottonwoods from which he could watch the town and he paused there momentarily. He saw what looked like three men on foot (but maybe they had horses stashed someplace nearby) and, coming out of the shelter of the trees, he made an even wider detour than he'd first planned.

Entering the town at last, he heard folks moving, somnolent sounds in a somnolent dawn.

He entered the place of his destination through a back door that was never locked, and he climbed some stairs, a narrow flight that was obviously not used much: this was no cathouse: folks who used it didn't need secret exits.

He went along a passage and he heard nothing. He halted at a door and knocked gently on its panels. There was the sound of movements inside and then a female voice called, "Come in."

He drew his gun, and then he opened the door with his other hand and walked through.

★ ★ ★

One of Ceegar's boys saw the horsemen approaching. "Not many," he said. "Four — five."

"Keep down," said Ceegar. "Let's wait an' take a better look at 'em."

"Two of 'em I know," said the second boy.

"Who do you think you are?" sported his pardner. "Chief All-Seeing-Sit-Ass-Bull?"

"Quit it," said Ceegar. "We know them. They're some of Dragoman's boys, even I can see that now."

"Then where is Dragoman?"

Ceegar grinned. "We'll take 'em. Mebbe they'll tell us."

They were in a disused outhouse adjacent to a hovel occupied by a crippled ex-miner who, as far as they knew, was still in bed. Everybody called him Cully. He'd had a nasty accident with some dynamite more than a while back and hadn't been the same man since.

The horsemen were almost upon the trio. They were riding like drifters who didn't have a care in the world. But then, as they got closer to the buildings, they underwent a subtle change. The watchers could then see their faces clearly, see their wariness mirrored in their eyes. But their heads were still on their horses' reins and now was the time for the others to move and Ceegar gave the signal with a brisk nod of the head.

The trio stepped out in the open and they bristled with guns.

"Stay, boys," said Ceegar. "One leetle move an' we'll pepper yuh, blow you to Kingdom Come."

One of them at least recognized him,

whispered his name. They sure as hell hadn't expected to see Ceegar here. And his boys, tough-looking specimens both, were loaded for bear.

"You can't stop us," said another man like a kid whose ma was standing between him and his pals and the cookies they desired.

"Don't be a foolish young man," Ceegar said mildly.

Then another voice spoke up behind him. Gruff, a little shaky.

"I should drop the guns if I wuz you, boys," the voice said.

Ceegar looked back over his shoulder. "'Mornin', Cully," he said.

"Mornin', Ceegar. Boys."

"Mornin', Cully," the two pardners chorused.

Then one of them went behind the horsemen and told them to climb down and then relieved them of their weapons.

"We'll need rope, Cully," Ceegar said. "An' rag to stuff their jaws with. I don't want to shoot any of 'em yet.

We still want to be as quiet as mice — an' them too."

"You'll have what you need, pardner," Cully said.

He sloped his double-barrelled shotgun and turned back to his door, walking lopsidedly, favouring his badly twisted left leg.

"Bring 'em in here," said Ceegar, indicating the outhouse he and the two boys had recently quitted.

They were shepherded, marched, made to sit down in a line against a perilously leaning, brittle log wall.

Cully returned with enough hemp to corral a team of wild horses, and something else which looked somewhat unmentionable but was probably an old horse-blanket, torn and filthy.

The old ex-miner insisted on helping the two boys to truss and gag the outlaws. Ceegar didn't object, knowing how cantankerous Cully got if he figured folks were favouring him because of his bad leg.

"We best get back in town," said

Ceegar. "Dragoman and others might've come in another way, although Bill Dakell an' the rest'll be keeping watch like Max said. I guess Max is about now."

Max was just getting up, in fact, and as far as he knew nothing had happened. He left the two boys at the law office, getting ready to relieve other watchers. He was popping in to see Nita whom he hadn't visited yet since he came back off the trail. It would be a very brief visit, he thought, but it would prevent her from coming looking for him and getting in the way of something.

Main Street was pretty quiet as he moved along it.

He suddenly realized that there was something more important he should do before he saw Nita. Yeh, sure, why hadn't he thought of it as soon as he got up; what was the matter with his damned head?

Anyway, Nita and he didn't seem lately to be as close as they used to be. They still went through the usual motions, but, somehow, there wasn't the same feeling . . .

She's getting restless, he had thought. Yeh, he knew how she felt. He felt that way himself pretty often. He could work off his restlessness in his work, the trail, the gunplay; but how could Nita work off hers?

He was abreast of the doctor's surgery and he turned sharply and went in, said 'Howdy' to a lady he knew, a patient. There weren't any more right then.

"Mornin', Max," the doc said.

"Mornin', Doc. How's the patient?"

"He's awake. He'll mend. He told me he wanted to see you. I figured you'd be calling anyway."

"Yeh. Can I go up?"

"I'll come with you."

The wounded man was propped up in bed. His voice was soft but he didn't seem to be feeling any pain. After the preliminary polite greetings, Hardisty, not the sort to go around the houses asked a blunt question.

223

"Who are you? You look kinda familiar to me, but . . . " He let the rest hang in the air.

The young man in the bed said, "Marshal, my name is Matthew Raithe. Everybody calls me just Matt — to separate me, sort of, from my elder brother, Ben, who had always been called just Raithe."

"Ben Raithe, yeh," said Hardisty. "Used to be foreman for that old reprobate Boyard who runs the spread near the Texas borderlands."

"My brother was still with Boyard — till Boyard got killed an' then Ben did also."

"How?"

"Starke Dragoman and his bunch. I was over in Texas, didn't know anything till I got back to the ranch. I got after Dragoman, got some of his boys, not him I don't think. I got hit too, though. The rest you know. I figured they were coming here. I wish . . . " The voice died away.

"That's enough," said the doctor.

Hardisty reached and grasped the young man's shoulder, let it go. "Rest easy, pardner," he said. "Dragoman will be taken care of, I promise you that."

"All right, Marshal." The voice was a whisper as, with the help of the doctor, the patient was eased down in the bed. And Hardisty left the room.

23

NITA faced Starke Dragoman in the room. He had pouched his gun and stood grinning at her, the scar livid on his dark face.

"I didn't bank on no killing," she said. "I didn't aim for that, as God's my witness, never . . ."

"Don't go religious on me, honey."

He was still grinning, lantern-jawed, scar-faced.

"I wish now I'd never run into you during that trip I took . . ."

"Too late for that now."

"I knew what was goin' to happen, the cattle comin' in, the money changing hands. Robbery, rustling. I didn't figure on no killing . . ."

"So you said before. But, like I said, it's too late now."

"I just saw a way for getting out of here. I'd've waited, taken my cut.

Nobody would've suspected me. I could've sold this place and then moved on, started afresh."

"Hardisty might have suspicioned."

"He wouldn't have. Not if I'd waited. I'd got it all planned. Besides, I think Max is cooling off. I think he's getting restless. Maybe he ain't cut out to be a lawman."

"He's a paid killer," said Dragoman. "Never been anything else. He's no better'n you an' me. Hell, woman, you knew what might happen, and it's no good trying to tell me you didn't."

She had known him a long time. Longer than she had known Hardisty. Longer than she had known Luke, who had been superseded by Hardisty. Luke and Starke, both outlaws, though she didn't think they had ever run into each other: she'd been on her own when she joined up with the bunch that were known as Luke and his Lads. Hell's bells, was that the only sort of thing she was cut out for after all?

She had known Starke just after his

two mentors had met their final come-uppance and he had taken their names for his own. He'd been a wild one all right. But not like he was now. In his way, he'd been good to her until he'd sent her on her way, had had to run to Mexico with the law at his heels.

Maybe the law had given up. That hadn't been New Mexico law anyway. She had heard about him since and, with the strange loyalty she still felt for him, hadn't believed a lot she heard.

Had she been passing through some rose-coloured dream for the while when she ran into him again while she was on a buying trip for the Superbe Hotel?

Why had she . . . ?

Questions!

She couldn't answer those questions. Seemed like she couldn't even seem to find anything else to say to him now, had dried up.

Maybe he felt the same. They stood staring at each other. They were still doing so when they heard the footsteps in the passage. Then the door was rapped.

Dragoman turned towards it and drew his gun.

The door was opened and Hardisty came in.

Dragoman pointed the gun.

Nita cried, "Max!"

She came from behind Dragoman, her arm looping, her hand grabbing his wrist and jerking, forcing the gun upwards as it went off, the man pressing the trigger almost in a reflex action. Dragoman swung around violently, his whole weight hitting Nita. She was knocked backwards as if by a battering ram.

The window was wide open behind her, curtains fluttering in the morning breeze and already the warm air comming through, presaging a hot and maybe stormy day. Nita was completely off-balance as she hit the window, the sill, her arms flailing. She screamed shrilly. Then she was gone.

Hardisty's gun was out. But he was

scared of hitting the girl. Then she was out of his sight, fallen to the hard ground at the back of the Hotel Superbe. Dragoman's first shot had missed its mark entirely and torn a groove in the door jamb. Hardisty fired now, but he missed too, and then Dragoman was too close, too fast, coming at him like a maddened bull.

Both men crashed against the edge of the door the door swinging, hitting their bodies, Hardisty twisting, out of balance. Then Dragoman was past him, haring along the hallway.

Hardisty righted himself, leaning against the wall, raising his gun. But then Dragoman was at the top of the stairs and soon out of sight. Hardisty went after him.

He was halfway down the stairs when he spotted his man again. Dragoman whirled around in the lobby, gun glinting in the morning sunshine streaming through a side window. The gun was levelled. Hardisty sat down on a step as if he needed a rest. The slug went over his head — and then Dragoman was almost at the door, and another man was coming through it, suddenly startled, wide-eyed.

Hardisty opened his mouth to shout, shut it again. The man sprawled on the inside of the door as the big outlaw charged him.

The fallen man was scrambling to his feet: he was mad now. Hardisty cursed and lowered his gun. Dragoman was out on the boardwalk, unseen.

Hardisty negotiated the rest of the stairs and ran across the lobby. The man by the door said 'Marshal'. Hardisty didn't know him very well, said nothing, went past him, crouching low, swinging through the door, gun pointed out in front of him.

Dragoman was on the other side of the street and there didn't seem to be anybody else around. Hardisty jack-knifed into a stoop on the boardwalk and the shot that the other man flung at him went over his head and smashed through the glass panel in top of the door behind him.

Hardisty rolled, sparsely covered by the hitching rack, which didn't yet hold a single horse. Hardisty levelled his gun. The sun came in at the side of him and, across from him, Dragoman was a tall, dark figure. He was standing his ground now.

Hardisty saw the lance of flame, the black smoke — even as he was thumbing the hammer of his own weapon, the heavy steel bucking in his hand. Chips of wood were slashed into his face from a post and the slug almost sliced his ear off: he heard the menacing buzz. He steadied his weapon. Then he saw that Dragoman was dropping.

The tall figure was foreshortening like the man was tired, wanted to lie down.

Then the man was turning, seeking cover and Hardisty stepped off the boardwalk and went forward. He pointed his gun as he strode on, straight, and he emptied the gun. It bucked satisfyingly in his hand, but not enough to make any difference.

The black smoke blew back into his face, making him squint his eyes. The sun's rays were getting stronger. But Hardisty could still see the black figure ahead of him; watching it crumple, watching it fall to a crumpled heap and then stretch out, look less.

Then he was standing over Dragoman, the empty gun in his hand, wisps of smoke still curling from its muzzle. And the man lying in his own blood on this boardwalk was still miraculously alive.

There was a wound in the side of his neck from which thick blood seeped. There seemed to be two holes in his chest and the redness was beginning to soak through his shirt. His long right arm was stretched downwards but the gun that that hand had clasped was unreachable now, lay off the edge of the dirty, splintered, heel-hammered planks. Dragoman's fingers were actually clutched at another wound in his groin as if somehow he felt that this was his most vulnerable place, this was the bad one. Blood ran through his fingers.

He looked up at Hardisty and his eyes were like hating orbs of fire as he whispered, "Damn you, Hardisty . . . Damn you . . . *Damn* . . ." Then his eyes closed, his breath rattled; he died.

Suddenly the street seemed full of people. Hardisty seemed to see them all very clearly.

Ranchers Dakell and Smithon. Texas Joe Elliwell with a bandage round his head. Jed Spokes and Aldo Boner. Hardisty's regular deputy Gil Tally, returned — sick relative mending hopefully. Tracker Moosehead, lop-sided, mending after being shot from his horse at the pass by Dragoman's snipers. Old Gabe, desk-clerk. Old Jack, hostler. Fat, bustling Mayor Mobane . . .

But the first folks to get to the marshal were Ceegar and his two boys, coming through the alley from the back, crossing the street quickly, then halting. Ceegar said, "We've got the others, Max."

Hardisty said, "Good . . . but Nita . . . The girl, how is she?"

Ceegar hadn't known Nita all that well, his boys not at all. "The doc's with her, Max," Ceegar said. "But he couldn't do any good. She hit her head on an old ruined ploughshare that's lyin' out there. Must've hit mighty hard. Must've finished her instantly, Max."

"Mercy!"

Hardisty had striven for answers. He figured he had them now — mostly.

He was a tough man. But he could be hurt. He'd carry that till it was gone from him. Didn't know how long that would take . . . Looked about him at all the people now. "Lot of cleaning up to be done," he said and it was as if he was talking to himself.

★ ★ ★

The dark-haired, blue-eyed girl called Annie stood in the middle of her vegetable garden with the chickens chattering in their pens behind her and looked out towards the narrow creek glittering in the sun and the sweeping plain beyond. She shaded her eyes with her hand to try and get a better look at the horse and rider who approached. The high-stepping horse. The tall rider erect in the saddle. Not coming fast, not with hurry. But coming straight. Becoming achingly familiar. So that the girl hoped, but then chided herself for doing so.

Just a horseman riding with the sun behind. A tall man riding out of the sun on a high-stepping steed.

And the girl, still shading her eyes with one hand, began to move slowly forward, avoiding her growing plants as if by instinct. But still staring outwards.

The horse began to splash through the creek and the rider raised one hand in a salute.

"Max," the girl cried. "Oh, God — Max."

And she moved faster. And then she began to run with both her hands held out before her.

THE END

Other titles in the
Linford Western Library:

TOP HAND
Wade Everett

The Broken T was big. But no ranch is big enough to let a man hide from himself.

GUN WOLVES OF LOBO BASIN
Lee Floren

The Feud was a blood debt. When Smoke Talbot found the outlaws who gunned down his folks he aimed to nail their hide to the barn door.

SHOTGUN SHARKEY
Marshall Grover

The westbound coach carrying the indomitable Larry and Stretch headed for a shooting showdown.

FIGHTING RAMROD
Charles N. Heckelmann

Most men would have cut their losses, but Frazer counted the bullets in his guns and said he'd soak the range in blood before he'd give up another inch of what was his.

LONE GUN
Eric Allen

Smoke Blackbird had been away too long. The Lequires had seized the Blackbird farm, forcing the Indians and settlers off, and no one seemed willing to fight! He had to fight alone.

THE THIRD RIDER
Barry Cord

Mel Rawlins wasn't going to let anything stand in his way. His father was murdered, his two brothers gone. Now Mel rode for vengeance.

ARIZONA DRIFTERS
W. C. Tuttle

When drifting Dutton and Lonnie Steelman decide to become partners they find that they have a common enemy in the formidable Thurston brothers.

TOMBSTONE
Matt Braun

Wells Fargo paid Luke Starbuck to outgun the silver-thieving stagecoach gang at Tombstone. Before long Luke can see the only thing bearing fruit in this eldorado will be the gallows tree.

HIGH BORDER RIDERS
Lee Floren

Buckshot McKee and Tortilla Joe cut the trail of a border tough who was running Mexican beef into Texas. They stopped the smuggler in his tracks.

BRETT RANDALL, GAMBLER
E. B. Mann

Larry Day had the choice of running away from the law or of assuming a dead man's place. No matter what he decided he was bound to end up dead.

THE GUNSHARP
William R. Cox

The Eggerleys weren't very smart. They trained their sights on Will Carney and Arizona's biggest blood bath began.

THE DEPUTY OF SAN RIANO
Lawrence A. Keating and
Al. P. Nelson

When a man fell dead from his horse, Ed Grant was spotted riding away from the scene. The deputy sheriff rode out after him and came up against everything from gunfire to dynamite.

FARGO: MASSACRE RIVER
John Benteen

The ambushers up ahead had now blocked the road. Fargo's convoy was a jumble, a perfect target for the insurgents' weapons!

SUNDANCE: DEATH IN THE LAVA
John Benteen

The Modoc's captured the wagon train and its cargo of gold. But now the halfbreed they called Sundance was going after it . . .

HARSH RECKONING
Phil Ketchum

Five years of keeping himself alive in a brutal prison had made Brand tough and careless about who he gunned down . . .

FARGO: PANAMA GOLD
John Benteen

With foreign money behind him, Buckner was going to destroy the Panama Canal before it could be completed. Fargo's job was to stop Buckner.

FARGO: THE SHARPSHOOTERS
John Benteen

The Canfield clan, thirty strong were raising hell in Texas. Fargo was tough enough to hold his own against the whole clan.

PISTOL LAW
Paul Evan Lehman

Lance Jones came back to Mustang for just one thing — revenge! Revenge on the people who had him thrown in jail.

HELL RIDERS
Steve Mensing

Wade Walker's kid brother, Duane, was locked up in the Silver City jail facing a rope at dawn. Wade was a ruthless outlaw, but he was smart, and he had vowed to have his brother out of jail before morning!

DESERT OF THE DAMNED
Nelson Nye

The law was after him for the murder of a marshal — a murder he didn't commit. Breen was after him for revenge — and Breen wouldn't stop at anything . . . blackmail, a frameup . . . or murder.

DAY OF THE COMANCHEROS
Steven C. Lawrence

Their very name struck terror into men's hearts — the Comancheros, a savage army of cutthroats who swept across Texas, leaving behind a bloodstained trail of robbery and murder.

SUNDANCE: SILENT ENEMY
John Benteen

A lone crazed Cheyenne was on a personal war path. They needed to pit one man against one crazed Indian. That man was Sundance.

LASSITER
Jack Slade

Lassiter wasn't the kind of man to listen to reason. Cross him once and he'll hold a grudge for years to come — if he let you live that long.

LAST STAGE TO GOMORRAH
Barry Cord

Jeff Carter, tough ex-riverboat gambler, now had himself a horse ranch that kept him free from gunfights and card games. Until Sturvesant of Wells Fargo showed up.

McALLISTER ON THE COMANCHE CROSSING
Matt Chisholm

The Comanche, McAllister owes them a life — and the trail is soaked with the blood of the men who had tried to outrun them before.

QUICK-TRIGGER COUNTRY
Clem Colt

Turkey Red hooked up with Curly Bill Graham's outlaw crew. But wholesale murder was out of Turk's line, so when range war flared he bucked the whole border gang alone . . .

CAMPAIGNING
Jim Miller

Ambushed on the Santa Fe trail, Sean Callahan is saved by two Indian strangers. But there'll be more lead and arrows flying before the band join Kit Carson against the Comanches.

GUNSLINGER'S RANGE
Jackson Cole

Three escaped convicts are out for revenge. They won't rest until they put a bullet through the head of the dirty snake who locked them behind bars.

RUSTLER'S TRAIL
Lee Floren

Jim Carlin knew he would have to stand up and fight because he had staked his claim right in the middle of Big Ike Outland's best grass.

THE TRUTH ABOUT SNAKE RIDGE
Marshall Grover

The troubleshooters came to San Cristobal to help the needy. For Larry and Stretch the turmoil began with a brawl and then an ambush.

WOLF DOG RANGE
Lee Floren

Will Ardery would stop at nothing, unless something stopped him first — like a bullet from Pete Manly's gun.

DEVIL'S DINERO
Marshall Grover

Plagued by remorse, a rich old reprobate hired the Texas Trouble-shooters to deliver a fortune in greenbacks to each of his victims.

GUNS OF FURY
Ernest Haycox

Dane Starr, alias Dan Smith, wanted to close the door on his past and hang up his guns, but people wouldn't let him.